Arthur Henry Bullen

Carols and Poems from the Fifteenth Century to the Present Time

Arthur Henry Bullen

Carols and Poems from the Fifteenth Century to the Present Time

ISBN/EAN: 9783744765954

Printed in Europe, USA, Canada, Australia, Japan

Cover: Foto ©Andreas Hilbeck / pixelio.de

More available books at **www.hansebooks.com**

CAROLS AND POEMS

FROM

THE FIFTEENTH CENTURY TO
THE PRESENT TIME

EDITED BY

A. H. BULLEN, B.A.

LONDON
JOHN C. NIMMO
14, KING WILLIAM STREET, STRAND, W.C.
1886

To my Wife.

When skies were blue and hearts were gay,
We wandered in the prime of May
By primrose-banks, and where the breeze
Shook snow-bloom from the cherry-trees,
And golden gorse stretched leagues away.

When August eves were cool and sweet,
We watched the slant rays gild the wheat,
Or far down woodland alleys lone
Heard stock-doves make delicious moan,
And chid the hours that flew so fleet.

Now, while the twinkling shadows fall
Athwart the casement and the wall,
Beside the fire-light's ruddy gleam,
As day goes down, we muse and dream,
And all our past delights recall.

Tho' envious mists usurp the morn,
And mire lies deep in ways forlorn,
Sweet Heart, while Love our feet shall guide,
What ills, forsooth, can us betide
Who laugh the darkling days to scorn?

Contents.

—o—

Part I.

CHRISTMAS CHANTS AND CAROLS.

CONTENTS.

Part II.

CARMINA SACRA.

Part III.

CHRISTMAS CUSTOMS AND CHRISTMAS CHEER.

preface.

---o---

IT is a commonplace with poets to lament over the
degeneracy of the times.   Even Homer thought
the world was in a parlous state, for he twits his coun-
trymen with their feebleness, protesting that two picked
men could hardly lift on to a waggon the stone which
Hector brandished with ease.   The aged ploughman
in Lucretius envies the fortune of his forefathers, who
gained a comfortable livelihood from a scanty patch of
ground; and the sorrowful vineplanter wearies Heaven
with his complaints, perceiving not (says the poet) that
all things little by little are wasting away by length of
days and faring towards the grave.   Evermore rises the
same wail over the poverty of present times, and evermore we look back wistfully to the past.   As one turns
the pages of Herrick's " Hesperides," how grey and
colourless appears the England of to-day!   We have
become so serious, so demure, so respectable; we are
resolved that the game of life is a desperately earnest
business; we read Mr. Shorthouse.   " I sing of May-
poles, hock-carts, wassails, wakes!" wrote Herrick.
Alack, *nous avons changé tout cela.*   Instead of dancing

with Julia round a May-pole, he would be expected to
attend a May-meeting at Exeter Hall.   Flush-cheeked,
curly-haired Robin Herrick at a May-meeting! After
such an experience he would never have called Devonshire "dull."   Country life, as depicted in the "Hesperides," appears to have been one perpetual round of
merry-making.   Morris dances, Whitsun ale, twelfth-tide
kings and queens, stool-ball, shearing-feasts, mummeries,
wassailings, shrovings, and the like, are the subjects of
the poet's song.   It is hard, very hard, in this last
quarter of the nineteenth century to realise the life that
Herrick led.   Perhaps on a closer view much of the
brightness of the vision would fade away ; but still we
can never banish the feeling that something has been
lost of the old delight in life, the old buoyancy and fresh-
ness that possessed men's hearts before the Puritans
gained the mastery.

Such reflections forcibly suggest themselves as Christmastide draws near.   We still twine the holly and we
still eat mince-pies.   In one or two colleges the boar's
head is still served up with mustard.   But who now-a-
days sets a swan on the Christmas board, or who a
sturgeon ?   Where will you find "the carcasses of three
fat wethers bruised for gravy to make sauce for a single
peacock " ? [1]   That delightful writer, Nicholas Breton,
in his "Fantasticks " (1626), brings vividly home to us
the Christmas festivities of the early seventeenth century :—"It is now Christmas, and not a cup of drink

---

[1] Massinger's "City Madam," ii. 1. (Credat Judæus!)

must pass without a carol; the beasts, fowl, and fish come to a general execution, and the corn is ground to dust for the bakehouse and the pastry : cards and dice purge many a purse, and the youth show their agility in shoeing of the wild mare : now, good cheer, and welcome, and God be with you, and I thank you :—and against the New Year provide for the presents :—the Lord of Misrule is no mean man for his time, and the guests of the high table must lack no wine : the lusty bloods must look about them like men, and piping and dancing puts away much melancholy : stolen venison is sweet, and a fat coney is worth money : pit-falls are now set for small birds, and a woodcock hangs himself in a gin : a good fire heats all the house, and a full alms-basket makes the beggar's prayers :—the maskers and the mummers make the merry sport, but if they lose their money their drum goes dead : swearers and swaggerers are sent away to the ale-house, and unruly wenches go in danger of judgment : musicians now make their instruments speak out, and a good song is worth the hearing. In sum it is a holy time, a duty in Christians for the remembrance of Christ and custom among friends for the maintenance of good fellowship. In brief I thus conclude it : I hold it a memory of the Heaven's love and the world's peace, the mirth of the honest, and the meeting of the friendly. Farewell." It is pleasant by the fireside to linger over such a description as that ; to try to realise the nut-brown mirth that reigned at Christmastide three centuries ago. Sir John Reresby has left

us an interesting account of how he used to observe Christmas. "I returned," he writes[1] in 1684, "to Thrybergh,
by God's mercy, in safety, to keep Christmas amongst
my neighbours and tenants. I had more company this
Christmas than heretofore. The four first days of the
new year all my tenants of Thrybergh, Brinsford, Denby,
Mexborough, Hooton Roberts, and Rotherham dined with
me ; the rest of the time some four-score of gentlemen and
yeomen with their wives were invited, besides some that
came from York; so that all the beds in the house and most
in the town were taken up. There were seldom less than
four-score, counting all sorts of people, that dined in the
house every day, and some days many more. On New
Year's Day chiefly there dined above three hundred, so
that whole sheep were roasted and served up to feed
them. For music I had four violins, besides bagpipes,
drums, and trumpets." Nobody could grudge broad
acres to a landowner who so well understood hospitality.
On another occasion,[2] in 1682, the festivities were on
a less lavish scale. There assembled on Christmas Eve
nineteen of the poorer tenants from Denby and Hooton ;
on Christmas Day twenty-six of the poorer tenants from
Thrybergh, Brinsford, and Mexborough ; on St. Stephen's
Day farmers and better sort of tenants to the number
of fifty-four ; on St. John's Day forty-five of the chief
tenants ; on the 30th of December eighteen gentlemen
of the neighbourhood with their wives ; on the 1st of
January sixteen gentlemen ; on the 4th twelve of the

[1] Memoirs of Sir John Reresby (Camden Society), p. 310.
[2] Ibid., pp. 266–7.

neighbouring clergymen; and on the 6th seven gentlemen and tradesmen. Among the guests who lay at the
house were "Mr. Rigden, merchant of York, and his
wife, *a handsome woman,*" and "Mr. Belton, an ingenious clergyman, but too much a good fellow." How
gentle is the censure conveyed in the words "too much
a good fellow!" Sir John adds: "The expense of
liquor, both of wine and others, was considerable, as
of other provisions, and my friends appeared well satis-
fied." So they ought to have been. But all landlords
were not like Sir John Reresby, and he tells us himself
that few of the gentry in his part of the country observed
the festival. Complaints of niggardly housekeeping
were constantly being made. In the "Roxburghe Collection" is a very doleful ballad entitled "Christmas'
Lamentation for the loss of his acquaintance, showing
how he is forced to leave the country and come to
London." Hear how it begins :—

> " Christmas is my name ; far have I gone,
>   Have I gone, have I gone, have I gone,
>   Without regard ;
>   Whereas great men by flocks there be flown,
>   There be flown, there be flown, there be flown,
>   To London ward ;
>   Where they in pomp and pleasure do waste
>   That which Christmas was wonted to feast,
>   Welladay !
>   Houses where music was wont for to ring,
>   Nothing but bats and howlets do sing,
>   Welladay, welladay, welladay !
>   Where should I stay ?

b

> Christmas beef and bread is turned to stones, &c.
>   And silken rags ;
> And lady Money sleeps, and makes moans, &c.
>   In misers' bags.
> Houses where pleasure once did abound,
> Nought but a dog and a shepherd is found,
>   Welladay !
> Places where Christmas revels did keep,
> Is now become habitations for sheep,
>   Welladay ! "

Poor Robin's Almanac harps perpetually on the same theme. Against such curmudgeons was directed the old carol of *Dives and Lazarus*, which must have been sung at many a rich churl's door to the gratification of a knot of shivering wretches. I give it from an old broadside [1] in the Bodleian.

> " As it fell out upon a day
>   Rich Dives made a feast,
> And he invited all his friends
>   And gentry of the best.
>
> Then Lazarus laid him down and down,
>   E'en down at Dives' door ;
> Some meat, some drink, brother Dives,
>   Bestow upon the poor.
>
> Thou art none of my brother, Lazarus,
>   That lies begging at the door.
> No meat nor drink will I give to thee,
>   Nor bestow upon the poor.

---

[1] Printed in the last century by T. Bloomer, 53 Edgbaston Street, Birmingham.

Then Lazarus laid him down and down,
   E'en down at Dives' wall;
Some meat, some drink, brother Dives,
   Or with hunger starve I shall.

Thou art none of my brother, Lazarus,
   That lies begging at my wall ;
For neither meat nor drink will I give,
   But with hunger starve you shall.

Then Lazarus laid him down and down
   E'en down at Dives' gate ;
Some meat, some drink, brother Dives,
   For Jesus Christ His sake.

Thou art none of my brother, Lazarus,
   That lies begging at my gate ;
No meat nor drink will I give to thee
   For Jesus Christ His sake.

Then Dives sent out his merry men,
   To whip poor Lazarus away,
They had no power to strike one stroke,
   But flung their whips away.

Then Dives sent out his hungry dogs
   To bite him as he lay ;
They had no power to bite at all,
   But licked his sores away.

As it fell out upon a day,
   Poor Lazarus sickened and died ;
There came two angels out of heaven,
   His soul therein to guide.

Rise up, rise up, brother Lazarus,
    And go along with me,
For you've a place prepared in heaven
    Upon an angel's knee.[1]

As it fell out upon a day,
    Rich Dives sickened and died ;
There came two serpents out of hell,
    His soul therein to guide.

Rise up, rise up, brother Dives,
    And go along with me ;
There is prepared a place in hell
    From which thou ne'er can flee.

Then Dives looked up with his eyes,
    And saw poor Lazarus blest ;
Give a drop of water, brother Lazarus,
    To quench my burning thirst.

O had I as many years to abide,
    As there are blades of grass,
Then there would be an end, but now
    Hell's pains will never pass.

O was I now but alive again,
    The space of one half hour ;
O that I'd made my peace secure,
    Then the devil should have no power ! "

Churls of the class of Dives will always exist, but one likes to think that there are fewer of them now than formerly. Truly, there is every need to-day for sympathy and charity towards the poor and the afflicted.

---

[1] Another copy reads :—
            " In angels' company."

Very pleasant is the obsolete practice of combining devotion and good fellowship. Fancy a modern rhymester hailing the arrival of Christmas after this style !—

> " Now that the time is come wherein
> Our Saviour Christ was born,
> The larders full of beef and pork,
> The garners filled with corn," &c.

Finding these verses in *Poor Robin's Almanac* for 1700, we are charmed by their quaint sincerity. Ah that homely piety and simple-hearted mirth might be revived ! These are dull times. Where are the mummers and the maskers ? Where the Lord of Misrule and the Twelfth-tide kings and queens ? What a poor business is a country-fair to-day ! Smock-races,[1] hot-hasty-pudding contests, and grinning through a horse-collar have been abolished. Merry-go-rounds and shooting-galleries are well-nigh the only attractions. But we must remember that, with many innocent diversions, not a few barbarous sports have been swept away. Cock-fighting still has its supporters in the Black Country, but it is to be hoped that nobody is anxious to revive cock-throwing or goose-riding. In remote districts many good old customs still linger. The wassailers still sing their cheery song, and the Christmas play, with its odd medley of characters, St. George,

---

[1] So called because the successful girl was presented with a holland smock.

the Turk, the Doctor, Beelzebub[1] (sometimes with the
addition of Oliver Cromwell and the Duke of Welling-
ton), still delights bucolic audiences. Hone, writing more
than half a century ago, anticipated that the practice
of singing Christmas carols would be abolished in the
course of a few years. His lugubrious prophecy has
happily not been fulfilled. "As I sat on a sunny bank,"
" I saw three ships come sailing in," "God rest you,
merry gentlemen," " Remember, O thou man," " The first
Nowell the Angel did say," and others, are still sung year
after year. But the more fantastic carols seem to be losing
ground. "Cherry-tree carol," the finest of all carols,
has been shorn of half its beauty by modern prudishness.
Every girl and boy should be taught the lovely stanzas
beginning, "As Joseph was a-walking" (p. 31). Never
were Christ's praises chanted in sweeter, clearer tones.
At the present day people are too refined (or should we
say—stolid ?) to appreciate such strange pieces of com-
position as "Holy Well," "The moon shines bright,"
and "The Carnal and the Crane." In the most
characteristic carols there is a pathetic wistful melody,
as though the singer were yearning to give utterance to
the thoughts that crowd his soul. Sometimes, as in the
carol beginning "I sing of a maiden" (p. 4), the accents
ring clear and sweet, without a flaw. At other times

---

[1] " Here come I, Beelzebub ;
  Under my arm I carry a club,
  Under my chin I carry a pan,
  Don't I look a nice young man ? "

the language is semi-articulate, woven of cloud-fancies,
dim as a half-remembered dream.   He must have had
true poetic feeling who wrote the following strange carol
of *The Seven Virgins :* [1]—

" All under the leaves, and the leaves of life,
    I met with virgins seven,
And one of them was Mary mild,
    Our Lord's mother of Heaven.

' O what are you seeking, you seven fair maids,
    All under the leaves of life ;
Come tell, come tell, what seek you
    All under the leaves of life ?'

' We're seeking for no leaves, Thomas,
    But for a friend of thine,
We're seeking for sweet Jesus Christ
    To be our guide and thine.'

' Go down, go down to yonder town
    And sit in the gallery,
And there you'll see sweet Jesus Christ,
    Nailed to a big yew-tree.'

So down they went to yonder town
    As fast as foot could fall,
And many a grievous bitter tear
    From the Virgin's eye did fall.

' O peace, Mother, O peace, Mother,
    Your weeping doth me grieve ;
I must suffer this,' he said,
    'For Adam and for Eve.'

---

[1] I have not been able to see an old copy of this piece, which
I have taken from an excellent collection of Christmas Carols
edited a few years ago by "Joshua Sylvester."

' O Mother, take you John Evangelist
　　All for to be your son,
And he will comfort you sometimes
　　Mother, as I have done.'

' O come thou, John Evangelist,
　　Thou'rt welcome unto me,
But more welcome my own dear Son
　　Whom I nursed on my knee.'

Then he laid his head on his right shoulder,
　　Seeing death it struck him nigh,—
' The holy Mother be with your soul,
　　I die, Mother dear, I die.'

O the rose, the gentle rose,
　　And the fennel that grows so green,
God give us grace in every place
　　To pray for our king and queen.

Furthermore for our enemies all
　　Our prayers they should be strong :
Amen, good Lord ; your charity
　　Is the ending of my song."

Sung on the crisp frosty road beneath the flying moon, that pathetic and fantastic strain might well stir the hearers' hearts with far-off wonder and awe. But for some time past it has been a growing practice to sing carols in churches instead of in the open air. Only the less poetical carols are in use, and the element of picturesqueness is fast vanishing. One of the most popular carols is the piece beginning "Good King Wenceslas looked out," written by the Rev. Dr. Neale. The language is poor and commonplace to the last degree.

Much has been written about the history of Christmas Carols, and I have no intention in this brief preface of minutely traversing the well-trodden ground. In England the practice of carol-singing appears to have first become widely spread in the 15th century. Many of the pieces collected from MSS. by the labour of Ritson, Wright, and Sandys belong to this early date. We are fortunate in possessing an ancient MS. copy of the *Carol of St. Stephen* (p. 33). Doubtless (in a somewhat altered shape) *The Carnal and the Crane*, *The Holy Well*, and *The Seven Virgins* belong to the 15th century; but no early copies of these pieces, whether in print or MS., are known to exist. The earliest printed collection was issued by Wynkyn de Worde in 1521. Only a fragment of it has descended; and in this fragment Hearne the antiquary found the original version of the famous Boar's Head Carol. A later collection, printed by Richard Kele, was issued about 1550. Specimens from this unique volume were printed in "Bibliographical Miscellanies," 1813, whence I have drawn the pieces beginning, "In Bethlehem that noble place" (p. 10), and "Lords and Ladies all by dene" (p. 12). Other books of so-called Christmas Carols were licensed for printing in the latter part of the 16th century ; but the pieces in these collections appear to have been hymns rather than carols. Early in the next century we find a genuine example of a carol, with music, (" Remember, O thou man ") in Ravenscroft's " Melismata," 1611. A few years afterwards an attempt to supplant

the old carols was made by William Slatyer in "Cer-
taine of David's Psalmes intended for Christmas Carols."
At a somewhat later date a few carols, though not of the
best kind, are found among the Roxburghe Ballads.   In
the second half of the last centry T. Bloomer, a Birmingham printer, did good service by printing in broadside
form all the traditional carols he could find.   Jemmy
Catnach, of Great Monmouth Street, Seven Dials, in the
second quarter of the present century, was zealous in
diffusing the knowledge of Christmas Carols.   As the
season comes round hawkers still call at villagers' doors
with wretchedly-printed slips ; but only a few of the old
traditional carols continue to circulate.

Alongside of the sacred carols sung in the open air,
flourished the jovial carols sung at Christmas feasts.   A
small black-letter collection of these pieces was published
in 1642 ; another appeared in 1661 ; a small undated
collection belongs probably to the same time ; a fourth
is dated 1688.   These tracts, belonging to the class of
books that are most easily thumbed out of existence, are
of the rarest possible occurrence.   The library of the
British Museum does not possess a copy of any of them ;
but luckily they are all in the Bodleian, bound together
in a small duodecimo volume which once belonged to that
"facete" (to use the term he applies to Democritus
Junior) and ingenious scholar, Antony-à-Wood, the
never-to-be-forgotten author of "Athenæ Oxonienses."
In the Long Vacation I spent some delightful hours in
making copious extracts from these curious tracts,

which few previous collectors appear to have examined. It may be that the reader will not find the same pleasure in these old rustic songs as I found. For in truth I was in the mood to enjoy everything. Returning after long absence to Oxford, I thought the old spires and domes had never looked so beautiful before. The studious hush of the Bodleian was charming after the noise of London streets. Before me lay the MS. catalogue, in a 17th-century hand, of the books which Robert Burton bequeathed to the library he loved so well; and as with reverence I turned the pages, the air seemed filling with the ghosts of grand old Oxford scholars, men who lived before the days of competitive examinations and pretentious sciolism; men who loved learning for its own sake, and whose whole life passed as a summer's day. Then the walk in the mellow evening-air with an old fellow student to Foxcomb Hill, and the draught of foaming ale in the inn parlour where I had spent so many jovial hours! But I return to Antony-à-Wood's collection of carols. The reader will perceive that they are genuine specimens of the songs that were sung in farm-houses by shepherds and ploughmen at Christmas feasts in the 17th century. Very touching is the gratitude of the poor fellows for being allowed the run of their teeth :—

> " Of delicates so dainty
> I see now here is plenty,
> Upon this table ready here prepared ;
> Then let us now give thanks to those

That all things friendly thus bestows,
Esteeming not this world that is so hard.

For of the same my master
Hath made me here a taster ;
The Lord above requite him for the same !
And so to all within this house
I will drink a full carouse,
With leave of my good master and my dame.

And the Lord be praised
My stomach is well eased,
My bones at quiet may go take their rest ;
Good fortune surely followed me
To bring me thus so luckily
To eat and drink so freely of the best."

Their stomachs were sharp-set, and we may be sure
they played a nimble knife and fork throughout the
whole twelve days.   Christmas comes but once a year,
so they made the best of their time and lustily trolled
the nut-brown bowl in honour of St. Stephen and St.
John.   One of the most interesting pieces is the New
Year's Carol (p. 205), sung by the shepherd, who comes
bringing mellow pippins as presents for his master's
children, points [1] for the farm-labourers, and pins for the
maids.   The verses bidding Farewell to Christmas are
lugubrious indeed ; but the honest fellows doubtless
found consolation in the thought that they would feast
again next year.

---

[1] Tagged laces that held up the breeches.

Those who spent their Christmas at their own fireside had also carols, but of a soberer sort. The following verses, which evidently cannot boast of a high antiquity, I heard in Berkshire :—

> "When I'm at school my father
>   Is working on the farm,
> The harvest he must gather
>   To keep us all from harm.
>
> My brother is at sea,
>   My sister's gone from home,
> She must in service be
>   Till merry Christmas come.
>
> We all shall meet together
>   On merry Christmas Eve ;
> We reck not wind or weather
>   While we our Christmas keep.
>
> All round the rodded (?) earth
>   Each one might chance to say,
> Since last we met in mirth
>   'Twas merry Christmas Day."

Rather a doleful ditty that; no mention of goose or mince·pies. At the same time I took down the following slight but pretty rhymes :—

> " Sing we all merrily,
>   Christmas is here,
> The day that we love best
>   Of days in the year.

> Bring forth the holly,
>   The box and the bay,
> Deck out our cottage
>   For glad Christmas Day.
>
> Sing we all merrily,
>   Draw round the fire,
> Sister and brother,
>   Grandson and sire."

It would be easy to write a long dissertation about Christmas ceremonies, for the materials are all to our hand. But as I have no desire to make a parade of cheap learning, I refer the reader to that elaborate and easy accessible work, Brand's "Popular Antiquities." For one who has neither the learning of Brand nor the light touch of Leigh Hunt, it would be impertinent to write at length on so trite a theme. The present volume lays little claim to research. It has been put together in idle moments, and is intended rather for the general reader than for scholars. The orthography of the older pieces has been modernised, but I have endeavoured in all cases to give, as far as possible, a correct text. It may perhaps be thought that a few more old carols should have been included in the First Part. I omitted without hesitation such pieces as "When Jesus Christ was twelve years old" (popular though it is), "The Lord at first had Adam made," "When Cæsar Augustus had rais'd a taxation," "When old father Jacob was ready to die," &c.; but I parted reluctantly from "Blessed be that maid Mary," "Mary mother, meek and mild," "Marvel not, Joseph, on Mary mild," and others. Some readers may be vexed at finding in the Second Part so well-known a poem as Milton's "Ode on the Nativity." I have no particular affection for the poem as a whole, though I greatly admire certain stanzas, and am not blind to the marvellous metrical skill displayed throughout. With the sacred text of Milton I dared not tamper. I felt that I must print the Ode in its integrity or not at all; and I chose the first course. In regard to Crashaw, whose transcendent merits I should be the last to dispute, I had less hesitation. His Hymn of the Nativity I give entire, but of the Hymn for the Epiphany I quote only the opening lines, for the latter part abounds with the most violent conceits. At the end of the volume I have added a few notes. There is a striking poem by Frederick Tennyson, "The Holy Tide," which I should like to have included; but it is far too long. With two stanzas from it I take leave of the reader :—

" The days are sad, it is the Holytide :
    The Wintermorn is short, the Night is long ;
So let the lifeless Hours be glorified
    With deathless thoughts, and echoed in sweet song :
And through the sunset of this purple cup
    They will resume the roses of their prime,
And the old Dead will hear us and wake up,
    Pass with dim smiles and make our hearts sublime !

The days are sad, it is the Holytide ;
    Be dusky mistletoes and hollies strown,

Sharp as the spear that pierced his sacred side,
   Red as the drops upon his thorny crown ;
No haggard Passion and no lawless Mirth
   Fright off the sombre Muse,—tell sweet old tales,
Sing songs as we sit bending o'er the hearth,
   Till the lamp flickers, and the memory fails."

PART I.

CHRISTMAS CHANTS AND CAROLS.

From the Coventry Mysteries.

In every place I shall tell this.

IN every place I shall tell this,
 Of a clean maid that God is born,
And in our likeness God now clad is,
 Mankind to save that was forlorn ;
His mother a maid as she was beforn,
 Not foul-polluted as other women be,
But fair and fresh as rose on thorn,
 Lily-white, clean with pure virginity.

A

*Printed in Ritson's Ancient Songs,
Sandys' Carols, etc. (from Sloane
MS., 2593, temp. Henry VI.)*

Welcome Yule.

Welcome Yule, thou merry man,
In worship of this holy day.

WELCOME be thou, heaven-king,
　　Welcome born in one morning,
Welcome for whom we shall sing,
　　Welcome Yule.

Welcome be ye, Stephen and John,
Welcome Innocents every one,
Welcome Thomas Martyr one,
　　Welcome Yule.

Welcome be ye, good New Year,
Welcome Twelfth Day, both in fere,[1]
Welcome saintès lef[2] and dear,
　　Welcome Yule.

---

[1] In fere = in company.　　[2] Lef = loved.

Welcome be ye, Candlemas,
Welcome be ye, Queen of Bliss,
Welcome both to more and less,
    Welcome Yule.

Welcome be ye that are here,
Welcome all and make góod cheer;
Welcome all, another year,
    Welcome Yule.

*From Wright's Songs and Carols,
(Warton Society. A collection
printed from Sloane MS. 2593,
temp. Henry VI.)*

J Sing of a Maiden.

I SING of a maiden
    That is makeless;[1]
King of all kings
    To her son she ches;[2]
He came also[3] still
    There his mother was,
As dew in April
    That falleth on the grass.
He came also still
    To his mother's bower,
As dew in April
    That falleth on the flower.
He came also still
    There his mother lay,

---

[1] Matchless.   [2] Chose.   [3] As.

As dew in April
  That falleth on the spray.
Mother and maiden
  Was never none but she ;
Well may such a lady
  God's mother be.

From Harleian MS. 5396 *(date circ.*
1500*). Printed in Sandys' Christmas Carols, and other collections.*

In Excelsis Gloria.

WHEN Christ was born of Mary free
    In Bethlehem in that fair citie,
Angels sungen with mirth and glee,
       In Excelsis Gloria !

Herdsmen beheld these angels bright
To them appearèd with great light,
And said, God's son is born this night,
       In Excelsis Gloria !

This King is comen to save kind
[Even] in Scripture as we find,
[There]fore this song have we in mind,
       In Excelsis Gloria !

[Then, dear] Lord, for thy great grace
[Grant us] in bliss to see thy face,
Where we may sing to thee solace,
       In Excelsis Gloria !

*Printed in Sandys' Christmas Carols,
and other collections.*

The First Nowell the Angel did say.

THE first Nowell the Angel did say
    Was to three poor Shepherds in the fields as
        they lay;
In fields where they lay keeping their sheep
In a cold winter's night that was so deep.
       Nowell, Nowell, Nowell, Nowell,
       Born is the King of Israel.

They looked up and saw a Star
Shining in the East beyond them far;
And to the earth it gave great light,
And so it continued both day and night.
               Nowell, etc.

And by the light of that same Star
Three Wise Men came from country far;
To seek for a King was their intent,
And to follow the Star wherever it went.
               Nowell, etc.

The Star drew nigh to the North-West,
O'er Bethlehem it took its rest,
And there it did both stop and stay
Right over the place where Jesus lay.

                   Nowell, etc.

Then did they know assuredly
Within that house the King did lie :
One enter'd in then for to see,
And found the Babe in poverty.

                   Nowell, etc.

Then enter'd in those Wise Men three
Most reverently upon their knee,
And offer'd there in his presence
Both gold, and myrrh, and frankincense.

                   Nowell, etc.

Between an ox-stall and an ass
This Child truly there, born he was;
For want of clothing they did him lay
All in the manger among the hay.

                   Nowell, etc.

Then let us all with one accord
Sing praises to our heavenly Lord,
That hath made heaven and earth of nought,
And with his blood mankind hath bought.

Nowell, etc.

If we in our time shall do well,
We shall be free from death and hell;
For God hath prepared for us all
A resting-place in general.

Nowell, etc.

*This and the next Carol are from Christ-
mas Carolles newely imprinted
(circ. 1550), of which only a fragment has come down. Our text is
taken from Bibliographical Miscellanies (Oxford, 1813).*

In Bethlehem that noble Place.

IN Bethlehem that noble place,
   As by prophecy said it was,
Of the Virgin Mary full of grace,
Salvator mundi natus est.
     Be we merry in this feast,
     In quo salvator natus est.

On Christmas night an angel it told
To the shepherds, keeping their fold,
That into Bethlehem with beasts wold
Salvator mundi natus est.
          Be we merry, etc.

The shepherdès were compassed right,
About them was a great light ;
Dread ye nought, said the angel bright,
Salvator mundi natus est.
          Be we merry, etc.

Behold to you we bring great joy ;
For why? Jesus is born this day ;
To us, of Mary, that mild may,
Salvator mundi natus est.

Be we merry, etc.

And thus in faith find it ye shall,
Lying poorly in an ox-stall.
The shepherds then lauded God all,
Quia Salvator mundi natus est.

Be we merry, etc.

A new Carol of our Lady.

LORDS and ladies all by dene [1]
    For your goodness and honour,
I will you sing all of a queen;
Of all women she is the flower.
    Nowell, Nowell, Nowell, Nowell,
    This said the angel Gabriel.

Of Jesse there sprang a wight,
Isay said by prophecy,
Of whom shall come a man of might,
From death to life he will us buy.
                Nowell, etc.

There came an angel bright of face,
Flying from heaven with full great light,
And said, Hail! Mary, full of grace,
For thou shalt bear a man of might.
                Nowell, etc.

---

[1] "All by dene" = forthwith.

Astonied was that lady free,
And had marvell of that greeting ;
Angel, she said, how may that be,
For never of man I had knowing ?
Nowell, etc.

Dread thou nothing, Mary mild,
Thou art fulfilled with great virtue,
Thou shalt conceive and bear a child
That shall be namèd sweet Jesu.
Nowell, etc.

She kneeled down upon her knee ;
As thou hast said, so may it be,
With heart, thought and mild cheer,
God's hand-maid I am here.
Nowell, etc.

Then began her womb to spring,
She went with child without man,
He that is lord over all thing,
His flesh and blood of her had than.[1]
Nowell, etc.

---

[1] Then.

Of her was born our heaven-king,
And she a maid never the less ;
Therefore be merry and let us sing,
For this new lord of Christmas.

Nowell, Nowell, etc.

From Songs and Carols, now first printed from a manuscript of the fifteenth century; Edited by Thomas Wright, 1847. (Percy Society Publications.)

The Virgin and Child.

THIS endris night [1]
    I saw a sight,
    A star as bright as day;
And ever among
A maiden sung,
    Lullay, by by, lullay.

This lovely lady sat and sang, and to her child [she]
    said—
" My son, my brother, my father dear, why liest thou
    thus in hayd?
    My sweet bird,[2]
    Thus it is betide
        Though thou be king veray;
But, nevertheless,
I will not cease
        To sing, by by, lullay."

---

[1] " Endris night "=last night.
[2] Often used as a term of endearment.—In the former line
"hayd"=hay.

The child then spake; in his talking he to his mother
    said—

"I bekid [1] am king, in crib though I be laid;
       For angels bright
       Down to me light,
          Thou knowest it is no nay,
       And of that sight
       Thou mayest be light
          To sing, by by, lullay."

"Now, sweet Son, since thou art king, why art thou
    laid in stall?

Why not thou ordain thy bedding in some great king's
    hall?
       Methinketh it is right
       That king or knight
          Should be in good array;
       And them among
       It were no wrong
          To sing, by by, lullay."

"Mary, mother, I am thy child, though I be laid in
    stall,

Lords and dukes shall worship me and so shall kingès
    all.

---

[1] *i.e.* it happens that I am king.

Ye shall well see
That kingès three
  Shall come on the twelfth day ;
For this behest
Give me thy breast,
  And sing, by by, lullay."

"Now tell me, sweet Son, I thee pray, thou art my
  love and dear,
How should I keep thee to thy pay [1] and make thee
  glad of cheer?
  For all thy will
  I would fulfil
   Thou weet'st [2] full well in fay,
  And for all this
  I will thee kiss,
   And sing, by by, lullay."

"My dear mother, when time it be, take thou me up
  aloft,
And set me upon thy knee and handle me full soft.
  And in thy arm
  Thou wilt me warm,
   And keep [me] night and day ;

---

[1] Content.   [2] Knowest.

B

If I weep
And may not sleep
  Thou sing, by by, lullay."

"Now, sweet Son, since it is so, all things are at thy
    will,
I pray thee grant to me a boon if it be right and skill,[1]
    That child or man,
    That will or can,
      Be merry upon my day ;
    To bliss them bring,
    And I shall sing,
      Lullay, by by, lullay."

---

[1] Fitting, reasonable.

From Wright's Songs and Carols
(Percy Society).

About the Field they piped full right.

Tyrle, tyrle, so merrily the shepherds began to blow.

ABOUT the field they piped full right,
   Even about the midst of the night;
Adown from heaven they saw come a light.
                              Tyrle, tyrle.

Of angels there came a company
With merry songs and melody.
The shepherds anon gan them espy.
                              Tyrle, tyrle.

Gloria in excelsis the angels sung,
And said who [how?] peace was present among
To every man that to the faith would long.
                              Tyrle, tyrle.

The shepherds hied them to Bethlehem
To see that blessed sun's beam;
And there they found that glorious stream.
                              Tyrle, tyrle.

Now pray we to that meek child,
And to his mother that is so mild,
The which was never defiled.

Tyrle, tyrle.

That we may come unto his bliss,
Where joy shall never miss;
That we may sing in Paradise.

Tyrle, tyrle.

I pray you all that be here
For to sing and make good cheer,
In the worship of God this year.

Tyrle, tyrle.

*Printed in Sandys' Christmas Carols
from Add. MS. 5165 (ancient
songs temp. Henry VII. and VIII.)*

Ꮪhis Endnes Night Ꭻ saw a Sight.

A H, my dear Son, said Mary, ah, my dear,
Kiss thy mother, Jesu, with a laughing cheer.

This endnes [1] night I saw a sight
All in my sleep,
Mary, that may, she sang lullay
And sore did weep;
To keep she sought full fast about
Her Son from cold.
Joseph said, Wife, my joy, my life,
Say what ye would.
Nothing, my spouse, is in this house
Unto my pay; [2]
My Son a king, that made all thing,
Lieth in hay.

Ah, my dear Son! &c.

---

[1] Last.   [2] Content.

My mother dear, amend your cheer
   And now be still;
Thus for to lie it is soothly
   My Father's will.
Derision, great passion,
   Infinitely,
As it is found many a wound
   Suffer shall I;
On Calvary that is so high
   There shall I be,
Man to restore, nailèd full sore
   Upon a tree.
          Ah, my dear Son! &c.

A very popular Carol, printed in many collections.

I saw Three Ships come Sailing in.

I SAW three ships come sailing in
  On Christmas day, on Christmas day;
I saw three ships come sailing in
  On Christmas day in the morning.

And what was in those ships all three
  On Christmas day, on Christmas day;
And what was in those ships all three
  On Christmas day in the morning?

Our Saviour Christ and his lady,
  On Christmas day, on Christmas day;
Our Saviour Christ and his lady,
  On Christmas day in the morning.

Pray whither sailed those ships all three
  On Christmas day, on Christmas day;
Pray whither sailed those ships all three
  On Christmas day in the morning?

O they sailed into Bethlehem
   On Christmas day, on Christmas day ;
O they sailed into Bethlehem
   On Christmas day in the morning.

And all the bells on earth shall ring
   On Christmas day, on Christmas day ;
And all the bells on earth shall ring
   On Christmas day in the morning.

And all the angels in heaven shall sing
   On Christmas day, on Christmas day ;
And all the angels in heaven shall sing
   On Christmas day in the morning.

And all the souls on earth shall sing
   On Christmas day, on Christmas day ;
And all the souls on earth shall sing
   On Christmas day in the morning.

Then let us all rejoice amain
   On Christmas day, on Christmas day ;
Then let us all rejoice amain
   On Christmas day in the morning.

A more modern version of the preceding Carol. Communicated by A. A. to "Notes and Queries," 3d series, iii. 7. It used to be sung in Mid-Kent.

As I sat under a Sycamore Tree.

AS I sat under a sycamore tree, a sycamore tree, a
    sycamore tree,
I looked me out upon the sea,
        A Christmas day in the morning.

I saw three ships a·sailing there, a-sailing there, a-sail-
    ing there,
The Virgin Mary and Christ they bare,
        A Christmas day in the morning.

He did whistle, and she did sing, she did sing, she did
    sing,
And all the bells on earth did ring,
        A Christmas day in the morning.

And now we hope to taste your cheer, taste your cheer,
    taste your cheer,
And wish you all a happy new year,
        A Christmas day in the morning.

From Byrd's Psalmes, Sonets, etc., 1588.

My sweet little Baby, what meanest thou to cry?

MY sweet little baby, what meanest thou to cry?
    Be still, my blessed babe, though cause thou
      hast to mourn,
Whose blood most innocent to shed the cruel king hath
    sworn ;
And lo, alas ! behold what slaughter he doth make,
Shedding the blood of infants all, sweet Saviour, for
    thy sake.
A King, a King is born, they say, which King this
    king would kill :
O woe and woeful heavy day when wretches have their
    will !
         Lulla, la lulla, lulla lullaby.

Three kings this King of kings to see are come from
    far,
To each unknown, with offerings great, by guiding of
    a star ;

And shepherds heard the song, which angels bright
    did sing,
Giving all glory unto God for coming of this King,
Which must be made away—King Herod would him
    kill ;
O woe and woeful heavy day when wretches have their
    will !

                  Lulla, &c.

Lo, lo, my little babe, be still, lament no more ;
From fury thou shalt step aside, help have we still in
    store :
We heavenly warning have some other soil to seek ;
From death must fly the Lord of life, as lamb both
    mild and meek :
Thus must my babe obey the king that would him
    kill ;
O woe and woeful heavy day when wretches have their
    will !

                  Lulla, &c.

But thou shalt live and reign, as sibyls hath foresaid,
As all the prophets prophecy, whose mother, yet a
    maid

And perfect virgin pure, with her breasts shall up-
    breed

Both God and man that all hath made, the son of
    heavenly seed :

Whom caitives none can tray, whom tyrants none can
    kill :

O joy and joyful happy day when wretches want their
    will !

Lulla, &c.

*Known as Cherry Tree Carol. Con-
cerning the text see notes.*

Joseph was an Old Man.

I.

JOSEPH was an old man,
  And an old man was he,
When he wedded Mary
  In the land of Galilee.

Joseph and Mary walked
  Through an orchard good,
Where was cherries and berries
  So red as any blood.

Joseph and Mary walked
  Through an orchard green,
Where was berries and cherries
  As thick as might be seen.

O then bespoke Mary,
  So meek and so mild,
Pluck me one cherry, Joseph,
  For I am with child.

O then bespoke Joseph,
    With words most unkind,
Let him pluck thee a cherry
    That brought thee with child.

O then bespoke the babe
    Within his mother's womb—
Bow down then the tallest tree
    For my mother to have some.

Then bowed down the highest tree
    Unto his mother's hand :
Then she cried, See, Joseph,
    I have cherries at command.

O then bespake Joseph,—
    I have done Mary wrong ;
But cheer up, my dearest,
    And be not cast down.

O eat your cherries, Mary,
    O eat your cherries now,
O eat your cherries, Mary,
    That grow upon the bough.

Then Mary plucked a cherry
　　As red as the blood;
Then Mary went home
　　With her heavy load.

II.

As Joseph was a-walking
　　He heard an angel sing:—
" This night shall be born
　　Our Heavenly King;

" He neither shall be born
　　In housen nor in hall,
Nor in the place of Paradise,
　　But in an ox's stall;

" He neither shall be clothed
　　In purple nor in pall,
But all in fair linen
　　As were babies all.

" He neither shall be rocked
　　In silver nor in gold,
But in a wooden cradle
　　That rocks on the mould.

" He neither shall be christened
    In white wine nor red,
But with fair spring water
    With which we were christenèd."

III.

Then Mary took her young son
    And set him on her knee:
I pray thee now, dear child,
    Tell how this world shall be.

O I shall be as dead, mother,
    As the stones in the wall;
O the stones in the streets, mother,
    Shall mourn for' me all.

Upon Easter-day, mother,
    My uprising shall be;
O the sun and the moon, mother,
    Shall both rise with me.

From Sloane MS. 2593. The MS. was printed in 1856 by Thomas Wright for the Warton Society.

Saint Stephen was a Clerk.

SAINT STEPHEN was a clerk
 In King Herod's hall,
And servèd him of bread and cloth
 As ever king befall.

Stephen out of kitchen came,
 With boar's head on hand,
He saw a star was fair and bright
 Over Bethlehem stand.

He kist[1] adown the boar's head
 And went into the hall :
" I forsake thee, King Herod,
 And thy workès all.

---

[1] Cast.

C

" I forsake thee, King Herod,
    And thy workès all ;
There is a child in Bethlehem born
    Is better than we all."

" What aileth thee, Stephen ?
    What is thee befall ?
Lacketh thee either meat or drink
    In King Herod's hall ?"

" Lacketh me neither meat ne drink
    In King Herod's hall ;
There is a child in Bethlehem born
    Is better than we all."

" What aileth thee, Stephen ?
    Art thou wode [1] or thou ginnest to breed ? [2]
Lacketh thee either gold or fee
    Or any rich weed ?" [3]

" Lacketh me neither gold nor fee,
    Ne none rich weed ;
There is a child in Bethlehem born
    Shall helpen us at our need."

---

[1] Mad.   [2] Upbraid.   [3] Dress.

" That is also sooth,[1] Stephen,
    Also sooth i-wis [2]
As this capon crowè shall
    That lieth here in my dish."

That word was not so soon said,
    That word in that hall,
The capon crew *Christus natus est*
    Among the lordès all.

" Riseth up, my tormentors,
    By two and all by one,
And leadeth Stephen out of this town,
    And stoneth him with stone."

Tooken they Stephen
    And stoned him in the way,
And therefore is his even
    On Christès own day.

---

[1] " Also sooth "=as true.   [2] Assuredly.

*First printed in Ravenscroft's Melismata,
Musical Phansies fitting the court, city,
and country humours* (1611).

Remember, O thou Man.

REMEMBER, O thou Man,
   O thou Man, O thou Man ;
Remember, O thou Man,
   Thy time is spent.
Remember, O thou Man,
How thou camest to me than,[1]
And I did what I can,
   Therefore repent.

Remember Adam's fall,
O thou Man, O thou Man ;
Remember Adam's fall
   From Heaven to Hell.
Remember Adam's fall,
How we were condemned all
To Hell perpetual,
   There for to dwell.

---

[1] Old form of *then*.

Remember God's goodness,
O thou Man, O thou Man;
Remember God's goodness
    And promise made.
Remember God's goodness,
How his only Son he sent
Our sins for to redress,
    Be not afraid.

The Angels all did sing,
O thou Man, O thou Man;
The Angels all did sing
    On Sion hill.
The Angels all did sing
Praises to our heavenly king,
And peace to man living,
    With right good will.

The Shepherds amazed was,
O thou Man, O thou Man;
The Shepherds amazed was
    To hear the Angels sing.
The Shepherds amazed was
How this should come to pass,
That Christ our Messias
    Should be our King.

To Bethlehem did they go,
O thou Man, O thou Man ;
To Bethlehem did they go,
　　This thing to see.
To Bethlehem did they go
To see whether it was so,
Whether Christ was born or no,
　　To set us free.

As the Angels before did say,
O thou Man, O thou Man ;
As the Angels before did say,
　　So it came to pass.
As the Angels before did say,
They found him wrapt in hay
In a manger where he lay,
　　So poor he was.

In Bethlehem was he born,
O thou Man, O thou Man ;
In Bethlehem was he born
　　For mankind dear.
In Bethlehem was he born
For us that were forlorn,
And therefore took no scorn
　　Our sins to bear.

In a manger laid he was,
O thou Man, O thou Man;
In a manger laid he was
    At this time present.
In a manger laid he was,
Between an ox and an ass,
And all for our trespass,
    Therefore repent.

Give thanks to God always,
O thou Man, O thou Man ;
Give thanks to God always
    With hearts most jolly.
Give thanks to God always
Upon this blessed day,
Let all men sing and say,
    Holy, Holy.

The most popular of Christmas Carols.

God rest you merry, Gentlemen.

G OD rest you merry, gentlemen,
　　Let nothing you dismay,
For Jesus Christ our Saviour
　Was born upon this day
To save us all from Satan's power
　When we were gone astray.
　　O tidings of comfort and joy,
　　　For Jesus Christ our Saviour was born on
　　　　Christmas day.

In Bethlehem in Jewry
　This blessed babe was born,
And laid within a manger
　Upon this blessed morn ;
The which his mother Mary
　Nothing did take in scorn.
　　　　　　　　O tidings, &c.

From God our Heavenly Father
   A blessed angel came,
And unto certain shepherds
   Brought tidings of the same,
How that in Bethlehem was born
   The Son of God by name.
               O tidings, &c.

Fear not, then said the angel,
   Let nothing you affright,
This day is born a Saviour
   Of virtue, power, and might ;
So frequently to vanquish all
   The friends of Satan quite.
               O tidings, &c.

The shepherds at those tidings
   Rejoiced much in mind,
And left their flocks a feeding
   In tempest, storm, and wind,
And went to Bethlehem straightway,
   This blessed babe to find.
               O tidings, &c.

But when to Bethlehem they came,
    Whereat this infant lay,
They found him in a manger
    Where oxen feed on hay ;
His mother Mary kneeling
    Unto the Lord did pray.
                O tidings, &c.

Now to the Lord sing praises,
    All you within this place,
And with true love and brotherhood
    Each other now embrace ;
This holy tide of Christmas
    All others doth deface.
                O tidings, &c.

This and the six following pieces have been frequently printed in broadside form, and in collections of Carols.

To=morrow shall be my Dancing Day.

TO-MORROW shall be my dancing day,
    I would my true love did so chance
To see the legend of my play,
    To call my true love to my dance.
Sing, oh! my love, oh! my love, my love, my love,
This have I done for my true love.

Then was I born of a Virgin pure,
    Of her I took fleshly substance;
Thus was I knit to man's nature,
    ' To call my true love to my dance.
                        Sing, oh! &c.

In a manger laid and wrapped I was,
    So very poor, this was my chance,
Betwixt an ox and a silly poor ass,
    To call my true love to my dance.
                        Sing, oh! &c.

Then afterwards baptized I was,
   The Holy Ghost on me did glance,
My Father's voice heard from above,
   To call my true love to my dance.
                Sing, oh! &c.

Into the desert I was led,
   Where I fasted without substance;
The Devil bade me make stones my bread,
   To have me break my true love's dance.
                Sing, oh! &c.

The Jews on me they make great suit,
   And with me made great variance,
Because they lov'd darkness rather than light,
   To call my true love to my dance.
                Sing, oh! &c.

For thirty pence Judas me sold,
   His covetousness for to advance;
Mark whom I kiss, the same do hold,
   The same is he shall lead the dance.
                Sing, oh! &c.

Before Pilate the Jews me brought,
    Where Barabbas had deliverance ;
They scourg'd me and set me at nought,
    Judged me to die to lead the dance.
                Sing, oh ! &c.

Then on the cross hanged I was,
    Where a spear to my heart did glance ;
There issued forth both water and blood,
    To call my true love to my dance.
                Sing, oh ! &c.

Then down to hell I took my way
    For my true love's deliverance,
And rose again on the third day
    Up to my true love and the dance.
                Sing, oh ! &c.

Then up to heaven I did ascend,
    Where now I dwell in sure substance,
On the right hand of God, that man
    May come unto the general dance.
                Sing, oh ! &c.

The Holy Well.

AS it fell out one May morning,
  And upon one bright holiday,
Sweet Jesus asked of his dear mother,
  If he might go to play.

To play, to play, sweet Jesus shall go,
  And to play pray get you gone;
And let me hear of no complaint
  At night when you come home.

Sweet Jesus went down to yonder town,
  As far as the Holy Well,
And there did see as fine children
  As any tongue can tell.

He said, God bless you every one,
  And your bodies Christ save and see:
Little children, shall I play with you,
  And you shall play with me?

But they made answer to him, No :
They were lords' and ladies' sons ;
And he, the meanest of them all,
Was but a maiden's child, born in an ox's stall.

Sweet Jesus turned him around,
And he neither laughed 'nor smiled,
But the tears came trickling from his eyes
Like water from the skies.

Sweet Jesus turned him about,
    To his mother's dear home went he,
And said, I have been in yonder town,
    As far as you can see.

I have been down in yonder town
    As far as the Holy Well,
There did I meet as fine children
    As any tongue can tell.

I bid God bless them every one,
    And their bodies Christ save and see :
Little children, shall I play with you,
    And you shall play with me ?

But they made answer to me, No :
They were lords' and ladies' sons ;
And I, the meanest of them all,
Was but a maiden's child, born in an ox's stall.

Though you are but a maiden's child,
  Born in an ox's stall,
Thou art the Christ, the King of heaven,
  And the Saviour of them all.

Sweet Jesus, go down to yonder town
  As far as the Holy Well,
And take away those sinful souls,
  And dip them deep in hell.

Nay, nay, sweet Jesus said,
  Nay, nay, that may not be;
For there are too many sinful souls
  Crying out for the help of me.

The Carnal and the Crane.

A S I pass'd by a river side,
    And there as I did reign,[1]
In argument I chanced to hear
    A Carnal[2] and a Crane.

The Carnal said unto the Crane,
    If all the world should turn,
Before we had the Father,
    But now we have the Son !

From whence does the Son come ?
    From where and from what place ?
He said, In a manger,
    Between an ox and ass !

I pray thee, said the Carnal,
    Tell me before thou go,
Was not the mother of Jesus
    Conceived by the Holy Ghost ?

---

[1] A corruption of *rein* = run.   [2] Crow ?

D

She was the purest Virgin,
   And the cleanest from sin ;
She was the handmaid of our Lord,
   And mother of our King.   .

Where is the golden cradle
   That Christ was rocked in ?
Where are the silken sheets
   That Jesus was wrapt in ?

A manger was the cradle
   That Christ was rocked in ;
The provender the asses left
   So sweetly he slept on.

There was a star in the West land,
   So bright did it appear
Into King Herod's chamber,
   And where King Herod were.

The Wise Men soon espied it,
   And told the king on high,
A princely babe was born that night
   No king could e'er destroy.

If this be true, King Herod said,
   As thou tellest unto me,

This roasted cock that lies in the dish
  Shall crow full fences [1] three.

The cock soon freshly feathered was
  By the work of God's own hand,
And then three fences crowèd he
  In the dish where he did stand.

Rise up, rise up, you merry men all,
  See that you ready be,
All children under two years old
  Now slain they all shall be.

Then Jesus, ah! and Joseph,
  And Mary, that was so pure,
They travelled into Egypt,
  As you shall find it sure.

And when they came to Egypt's land,
  Amongst those fierce wild beasts,
Mary, she being weary,
  Must needs sit down to rest.

Come sit thee down, says Jesus,
  Come sit thee down by me,
And thou shalt see how these wild beasts
  Do come and worship me.

---

[1] Rounds.

First came the lovely lion,
    Which Jesu's grace did spring,
And of the wild beasts in the field,
    The lion shall be the king.

We'll choose our virtuous princes,
    Of birth and high degree,
In every sundry nation,
    Where'er we come and see.

Then Jesus, ah! and Joseph,
    And Mary, that was unknown,
They travelled by a husbandman,
    Just while his seed was sown.

God speed thee, man! said Jesus,
    Go fetch thy ox and wain,
And carry home thy corn again,
    Which thou this day hast sown.

The husbandman fell on his knees,
    Even before his face;
Long time hast thou been looked for,
    But now thou art come at last.

And I myself do now believe
Thy name is Jesus called;
Redeemer of mankind thou art,
Though undeserving all.

The truth, man, thou hast spoken,
Of it thou may'st be sure,
For I must lose my precious blood
For thee and thousands more.

If any one should come this way,
And inquire for me alone,
Tell them that Jesus passed by,
As thou thy seed did sow.

After that there came King Herod,
With his train so furiously,
Inquiring of the husbandman,
Whether Jesus passed by.

Why, the truth it must be spoke,
And the truth it must be known,
For Jesus passed by this way
When my seed was sown.

But now I have it reapen,
   And some laid on my wain,
Ready to fetch and carry
   Into my barn again.

Turn back, says the Captain,
   Your labour and mine's in vain,
It's full three quarters of a year
   Since he his seed has sown.

So Herod was deceivèd
   By the work of God's own hand,
And further he proceeded
   Into the Holy Land.

There's thousands of children young,
   Which for his sake did die,
Do not forbid those little ones,
   And do not them deny.

The truth now I have spoken,
   And the truth now I have shown
Even the blessed Virgin,
   She's now brought forth a Son.

Joys Seven.

THE first good joy our Mary had,
 It was the joy of one,
To see her own Son Jesus
 To suck at her breast bone ;
To suck at her breast bone,
 Good man, and blessed may he be,
Both Father, Son, and Holy Ghost,
 And Christ to eternity.

The next good joy our Mary had,
 It was the joy of two,
To see her own Son Jesus
 To make the lame to go ;
To make the lame to go,
     Good man, &c.

The next good joy our Mary had,
 It was the joy of three,

To see her own Son Jesus
　To make the blind to see;
To make the blind to see,
　　　　　Good man, &c.

The next good joy our Mary had,
　It was the joy of four,
To see her own Son Jesus
　To read the Bible o'er;
To read the Bible o'er,
　　　　　Good man, &c.

The next good joy our Mary had,
　It was the joy of five,
To see her own Son Jesus
　To raise the dead alive;
To raise the dead alive,
　　　　　Good man, &c.

The next good joy our Mary had,
　It was the joy of six,
To see her own Son Jesus
　To wear the crucifix;
To wear the crucifix,
　　　　　Good man, &c.

The next good joy our Mary had,
　It was the joy of seven,
To see her own Son Jesus
　To wear the crown of Heaven ;
To wear the crown of Heaven,
　Good man, and blessed may he be,
Both Father, Son, and Holy Ghost,
　And Christ to eternity.

The Moon Shines Bright.

THE moon shines bright, and the stars give a light
  A little before it was day,
Our Lord, our God, he called on us,
  And bid us awake and pray.

Awake, awake, good people all,
  Awake, and you shall hear,
Our Lord, our God, died on the cross,
  For us whom he loved so dear.

O fair, O fair Jerusalem,
  When shall I come to thee?
When shall my sorrows have an end,
  Thy joy that I may see?

The fields were green as green could be,
  When from his glorious seat
Our Lord, our God, he watered us,
  With his heavenly dew so sweet.

And for the saving of our souls
  Christ died upon the cross ;
We ne'er shall do for Jesus Christ
  As he has done for us.

The life of man is but a span,
  And cut down in its flower ;
We are here to-day and to-morrow are gone,
  We are all dead in an hour.

O pray teach your children, man,
  The while that you are here ;
It will be better for your souls
  When your corpse lies on the bier.

To-day you may be alive, dear man,
  Worth many a thousand pound ;
To-morrow may be dead, dear man,
  And your body be laid under ground.

With one turf at your head, O man,
  And another at your feet,
Thy good deeds and thy bad, O man,
  Will all together meet.

My song is done, I must be gone,
    I can stay no longer here.
God bless you all, both great and small,
    And send you a happy new year !

A Virgin most Pure.

A VIRGIN most pure, as the Prophets do tell,
　　Hath brought forth a Babe, as it hath befell,
To be our Redeemer from death, hell, and sin,
Which by Adam's transgression hath wrapt us all in.
　　Rejoice, and be you merry, set sorrow aside,
　　Christ Jesus our Saviour was born on this tide.

In Bethlehem city, in Jewry it was,
Where Joseph and Mary together did pass,
And there to be taxed, with many one mo,[1]
For Cæsar commanded the same should be so.
　　　　　　　　Rejoice, and be you merry, &c.

But when they had entered the city so fair,
The number of people so mighty was there,
That Joseph and Mary, whose substance was small,
Could get in the city no lodging at all.
　　　　　　　　Rejoice, &c.

---

[1] More.

Then they were constrained in a stable to lie,
Where oxen and asses they used to tie;
Their lodging so simple, they held it no scorn,
But against the next morning our Saviour was
    born.

                                    Rejoice, &c.

The King of all glory to the world being brought,
Small store of fine linen to wrap him was brought;
When Mary had swaddled her young Son so sweet,
Within an ox manger she laid him to sleep.

                                    Rejoice, &c.

Then God sent an angel from heaven so high,
To certain poor shepherds in fields where they lie,
And bid them no longer in sorrow to stay,
Because that our Saviour was born on this day.

                                    Rejoice, &c.

Then presently after, the shepherds did spy
A number of angels appear in the sky,
Who joyfully talked, and sweetly did sing,
To God be all glory, our Heavenly King.

                                    Rejoice, &c.

Three certain wise princes, they thought it most meet
To lay their rich offerings at our Saviour's feet ;
Then the shepherds consented, and to Bethlehem did
     go,
And when they came thither, they found it was so.
                    Rejoice, &c.

The Saviour of all People.

GOD bless the master of this house,
　　And all that are therein,
And to begin this Christmas tide
　　With mirth now let us sing.
　　　For the Saviour of all people
　　　　Upon this time was born,
　　　Who did from death deliver us,
　　　　When we were left forlorn.

Then let us all most merry be,
　　And sing with cheerful voice,
For we have good occasion now
　　This time for to rejoice.
　　　　　　　　For, &c.

Then put away contention all,
　　And fall no more at strife,
Let every man with cheerfulness
　　Embrace his loving wife.
　　　　　　　　For, &c.

With plenteous food your houses store,
 Provide some wholesome cheer,
And call your friends together
 That live both far and near.

> For, &c.

Then let us all most merry be,
 Since that we are come here,
And we do hope before we part
 To taste some of your beer.

> For, &c.

Your beer, your beer, your Christmas beer,
 That seems to be so strong,
And we do wish that Christmas tide
 Was twenty times so long.

> For, &c.

Then sing with voices cheerfully,
 For Christ this time was born,
Who did from death deliver us,
 When we were left forlorn.

> For, &c.

E

By Robert Herrick.

A Christmas Carol.

SUNG TO THE KING IN THE PRESENCE AT WHITEHALL.

Chor.—WHAT sweeter music can we bring,
        Than a carol, for to sing
The birth of this our heavenly King?
Awake the voice! awake the string!
Heart, ear, and eye, and everything
Awake! the while the active finger
Runs divisions with the singer.

From the flourish they come to the song.

Dark and dull night, fly hence away,
And give the honour to this day,
That sees December turn'd to May.

If we may ask the reason, say
The why and wherefore all things here
Seem like the spring-time of the year?

Why does the chilling winter's morn
Smile like a field beset with corn?
Or smell like to a mead new-shorn,
Thus on the sudden?   Come and see
The cause why things thus fragrant be:
'Tis he is born whose quickening birth
Gives life and lustre public mirth
To heaven and the under-earth.

Chor.—We see him come, and know him ours,
Who with his sunshine and his showers
Turns all the patient ground to flowers.

The darling of the world is come,
And fit it is we find a room
To welcome him.   The nobler part
Of all the house here, is the heart.

Chor.—Which we will give him; and bequeath
This holly and this ivy wreath,
To do him honour; who's our King,
And Lord of all this revelling.

*Printed in Ritson's Ancient Songs and
Ballads, Sandys' Christmas Carols,
etc. (from Harl. MS. 5396, temp.
Henry VI.)*

The Contest of the Ivy and the Holly.

N AY, ivy, nay,
  It shall not be, i-wis [1];
Let holly have the mastery
 As the manner is.

Holly stand in the hall,
 Fair to behold;
Ivy stand without the door
 She is full sore a-cold.
     Nay, ivy, nay, &c.

Holly and his merry men,
 They dancen and they sing;
Ivy and her maidens,
 They weepen and they wring.
     Nay, ivy, nay, &c.

---

[1] Assuredly.

Ivy hath a kybe,[1]
    She caught it with the cold;
So mot[2] they all have ae,[3]
    That with ivy hold.
        Nay, ivy, nay, &c.

Holly hath berries
    As red as any rose,
The foster[4] [and] the hunters
    Keep them from the doe[s].
        Nay, ivy, nay, &c.

Ivy hath berries
    As black as any sloe;
There come the owl
    And eat him as she go.
        Nay, ivy, nay, &c.

Holly hath birdès,
    A full fair flock,
The nightingale, the popinjay,
    The gentle laverock.
        Nay, ivy, nay, &c.

---

[1] The MS. has "lybe."—"Kybe" = chapped skin.
[2] May.   [3] Each, severally.   [4] Forester.

Good ivy,
    What birdès hast thou ?
None but the howlet
    That krey [1] "how, how."

Nay, ivy, nay,
    It shall not be, i-wis ;
Let holly have the mastery
    As the manner is.

---

[1] Cries.

By Robert Stephen Hawker.

Modryb Marya—Aunt Mary.

A CHRISTMAS CHANT.

In old and simple-hearted Cornwall, the household names " Uncle "
and " Aunt " were uttered and used as they are to this day in
many countries of the East, not only as phrases of kindred, but
as words of kindly greeting and tender respect.   It was in the
spirit, therefore, of this touching and graphic usage, that they
were wont on the Tamar side to call the Mother of God in their
loyal language *Modryb Marya*, or Aunt Mary.

NOW of all the trees by the king's highway,
    Which do you love the best?
O ! the one that is green upon Christmas Day,
    The bush with the bleeding breast.
Now the holly with her drops of blood for me :
For that is our dear Aunt Mary's tree.

Its leaves are sweet with our Saviour's Name,
    'Tis a plant that loves the poor :
Summer and winter it shines the same
    Beside the cottage door.
O ! the holly with her drops of blood for me :
For that is our kind Aunt Mary's tree.

'Tis a bush that the birds will never leave :
   They sing in it all day long ;
But sweetest of all upon Christmas Eve
   Is to hear the robin's song.
'Tis the merriest sound upon earth and sea :
For it comes from our own Aunt Mary's tree.

So, of all that grow by the king's highway,
   I love that tree the best ;
'Tis a bower for the birds upon Christmas Day,
   The bush of the bleeding breast.
O ! the holly with her drops of blood for me :
For that is our sweet Aunt Mary's tree.

1838.

By Robert Stephen Hawker.

The Child Jesus.

A CORNISH CAROL.

WELCOME that star in Judah's sky,
   That voice o'er Bethlehem's palmy glen :
The lamp far sages hailed on high,
   The tones that thrilled the shepherd men :
Glory to God in loftiest heaven !
   Thus angels smote the echoing chord ;
Glad tidings unto man forgiven,
   Peace from the presence of the Lord.

The Shepherds sought that birth divine,
   The Wise Men traced their guided way ;
There, by strange light and mystic sign,
   The God they came to worship lay.
A human Babe in beauty smiled,
   Where lowing oxen round him trod :
A maiden clasped her Awful Child,
   Pure offspring of the breath of God.

Those voices from on high are mute,
   The star the Wise Men saw is dim ;
But hope still guides the wanderer's foot,
   And faith renews the angel hymn :
Glory to God in loftiest heaven !
   Touch with glad hand the ancient chord ;
Good tidings unto man forgiven,
   Peace from the presence of the Lord.

1840.

By S. T. Coleridge.

The Shepherds went their hasty Way.

THE shepherds went their hasty way,
   And found the lowly stable-shed
Where the Virgin-Mother lay;
   And now they checked their eager tread,
For to the Babe that at her bosom clung,
A mother's song the Virgin-Mother sung.

They told her how a glorious light,
   Streaming from a heavenly throng,
Around them shone, suspending night!
   While sweeter than a mother's song,
Blest angels heralded the Saviour's birth,
Glory to God on high! and peace on earth!

She listened to the tale divine,
   And closer still the Babe she prest;
And while she cried, the Babe is mine!
   The milk rushed faster to her breast:

Joy rose within her like a summer's morn;
Peace, peace on earth! the Prince of peace is
　　born.

Thou Mother of the Prince of peace,
　　Poor, simple, and of low estate!
That strife should vanish, battle cease,
　　O why should this thy soul elate?
Sweet music's loudest note, the poet's story,—
Didst thou ne'er love to hear of fame and glory?

And is not War a youthful king,
　　A stately hero clad in mail?
Beneath his footsteps laurels spring;
　　Him earth's majestic monarchs hail
Their friend, their playmate! and his bold bright eye
Compels the maiden's love-confessing sigh.

"Tell this in some more courtly scene,
　　To maids and youths in robes of state!
I am a woman poor and mean,
　　And therefore is my soul elate:
War is a ruffian all with guilt defiled,
That from the aged father tears his child.

" A murderous fiend by fiends adored,
  He kills the sire and starves the son ;
The husband kills and from her board
  Steals all his widow's toil had won ;
Plunders God's world of beauty ; rends away
All safety from the night, all comfort from the day.

" Then wisely is my soul elate,
  That strife should vanish, battle cease ;
I'm poor and of a low estate,
  The Mother of the Prince of peace.
Joy rises in me, like a summer's morn :
Peace, peace on earth ! the Prince of peace is
    born ! "

By Miss Christina G. Rossetti.

A Christmas Carol.

IN the bleak mid-winter
  Frosty wind made moan,
Earth stood hard as iron,
  Water like a stone;
Snow had fallen, snow on snow,
  Snow on snow,
In the bleak mid-winter
  Long ago.

Our God, heaven cannot hold him,
  Nor earth sustain;
Heaven and earth shall flee away
  When he comes to reign:
In the bleak mid-winter
  A stable-place sufficed
The Lord God Almighty,
  Jesus Christ.

Enough for him whom cherubim
　Worship night and day,
A breastful of milk
　And a mangerful of hay;
Enough for him whom angels
　Fall down before,
The ox and ass and camel
　Which adore.

Angels and archangels
　May have gathered there,
Cherubim and seraphim
　Thronged the air; .
But only his mother,
　In her maiden bliss,
Worshipped the Beloved
　With a kiss.

What can I give him,
　Poor as I am?
If I were a shepherd
　I would bring a lamb,
If I were a wise man
　I would do my part,—
Yet what I can I give him,
　Give my heart.

*By Mr. William Morris (from Sedding's
Antient Christmas Carols, 1860).*

Masters, in this Hall.

"TO Bethlem did they go, the shepherds three ;
    To Bethlem did they go to see whe'r it were so
        or no,
    Whether Christ were born or no
    To set men free."

Masters, in this hall,
    Hear ye news to-day
Brought over sea,
    And ever I you pray.
      Nowell ! Nowell ! Nowell ! Nowell !
        Sing we clear !
      Holpen are all folk on earth,
        Born is God's Son so dear.

Going over the hills,
    Through the milk-white snow,
Heard I ewes bleat
    While the wind did blow.
           Nowell, etc.

Shepherds many an one
   Sat among the sheep ;
No man spake more word
   Than they had been asleep.
                     Nowell, etc.

Quoth I " Fellows mine,
   Why this guise sit ye?
Making but dull cheer,
   Shepherds though ye be?
                     Nowell, etc.

" Shepherds should of right
   Leap and dance and sing ;
Thus to see ye sit
   Is a right strange thing."
                     Nowell, etc.

Quoth these fellows then,
   "To Bethlem town we go,
To see a Mighty Lord
   Lie in manger low."
                     Nowell, etc.

F

" How name ye this Lord,
    Shepherds?" then said I.
"Very God," they said,
    "Come from Heaven high."

                        Nowell, etc.

Then to Bethlem town
    We went two and two,
And in a sorry place
    Heard the oxen low.

                        Nowell, etc.

Therein did we see
    A sweet and goodly May,
And a fair old man ;
    Upon the straw she lay.

                        Nowell, etc.

And a little CHILD
    On her arm had she ;
"Wot ye who this is?"
    Said the hinds to me.

                        Nowell, etc.

Ox and ass him know,
 Kneeling on their knee :
Wondrous joy had I
 This little BABE to see.
Nowell, etc.

This is CHRIST the Lord,
 Masters, be ye glad !
Christmas is come in,
 And no folk should be sad.
Nowell, etc.

*From Mr. William Morris's Land
East of the Sun and West of the
Moon (Earthly Paradise, vol. iii.)*

Outlanders, whence come ye last?

OUTLANDERS, whence come ye last?
  The snow in the street and the wind on the door.
Through what green sea and great have ye past?
Minstrels and maids, stand forth on the floor.

From far away, O masters mine,
  The snow in the street and the wind on the door.
We come to bear you goodly wine :
Minstrels and maids, stand forth on the floor.

From far away we come to you,
  The snow in the street and the wind on the door.
To tell of great tidings strange and true :
Minstrels and maids, stand forth on the floor.

News, news of the Trinity,
The snow in the street and the wind on the door.
And Mary and Joseph from over the sea :
Minstrels and maids, stand forth on the floor.

For as we wandered far and wide,
The snow in the street and the wind on the door.
What hap do ye deem there should us betide?
Minstrels and maids, stand forth on the floor.

Under a bent when the night was deep,
The snow in the street and the wind on the door.
There lay three shepherds tending their sheep :
Minstrels and maids, stand forth on the floor.

" O ye shepherds, what have ye seen,
The snow in the street and the wind on the door.
To slay your sorrow and heal your teen? "
Minstrels and maids, stand forth on the floor.

" In an ox-stall this night we saw,
The snow in the street and the wind on the door.
A Babe and a maid without a flaw.
Minstrels and maids, stand forth on the floor.

"There was an old man there beside,
  The snow in the street and the wind on the door.
His hair was white, and his hood was wide.
  Minstrels and maids, stand forth on the floor.

"And as we gazed this thing upon,
  The snow in the street and the wind on the door.
Those twain knelt down to the Little One.
  Minstrels and maids, stand forth on the floor.

"And a marvellous song we straight did hear,
  The snow in the street and the wind on the door.
That slew our sorrow and healed our care."
  Minstrels and maids, stand forth on the floor.

News of a fair and a marvellous thing,
  The snow in the street and the wind on the door.
Nowell, nowell, nowell, we sing!
  Minstrels and maids, stand forth on the floor.

From Mr. A. C. Swinburne's Poems
and Ballads (first series).

Three Damsels in the Queen's Chamber.[1]

THREE damsels in the queen's chamber,
  The queen's mouth was most fair ;
She spake a word of God's mother
  As the combs went in her hair.
      Mary that is of might,
      Bring us to thy Son's sight.

They held the gold combs out from her
  A span's length off her head ;
She sang this song of God's mother
  And of her bearing-bed.
      Mary most full of grace,
      Bring us to thy Son's face.

When she sat at Joseph's hand,
  She looked against her side ;

---

[1] Suggested by a drawing of Mr. D. G. Rossetti's.

And either way from the short silk band
  Her girdle was all wried.
      Mary that all good may,
      Bring us to thy Son's way.

Mary had three women for her bed,
  The twain were maidens clean ;
The first of them had white and red,
  The third had riven green.
      Mary that is so sweet,
      Bring us to thy Son's feet.

She had three women for her hair,
  Two were gloved soft and shod ;
The third had feet and fingers bare,
  She was the likest God.
      Mary that wieldeth land,
      Bring us to thy Son's hand.

She had three women for her ease,
  The twain were good women ;
The first two were the two Maries,
  The third was Magdalen.
      Mary that perfect is,
      Bring us to thy Son's kiss.

Joseph had three workmen in his stall,
   To serve him well upon;
The first of them were Peter and Paul,
   The third of them was John.
      Mary, God's handmaiden,
      Bring us to thy Son's ken.

"If your child be none other man's,
   But if it be very mine,
The bedstead shall be gold two spans,
   The bed-foot silver fine."
      Mary that made God mirth,
      Bring us to thy Son's birth.

"If the child be some other man's,
   And if it be none of mine,
The manger shall be straw two spans,
   Betwixen kine and kine."
      Mary that made sin cease,
      Bring us to thy Son's peace.

Christ was born upon this wise,
   It fell on such a night,
Neither with sounds of psalteries,
   Nor with fire for light.
      Mary that is God's spouse,
      Bring us to thy Son's house.

The star came out upon the east
　　With a great sound and sweet :
Kings gave gold to make him feast
　　And myrrh for him to eat.
　　　　　Mary, of thy sweet mood,
　　　　　Bring us to thy Son's good.

He had two handmaids at his head,
　　One handmaid at his feet ;
The twain of them were fair and red,
　　The third one was right sweet.
　　　　　Mary that is most wise,
　　　　　Bring us to thy Son's eyes.　　Amen.

PART II.

CARMINA SACRA.

By John Milton.

On the Morning of Christ's Nativity.

THIS is the month, and this the happy morn,
　Wherein the Son of Heaven's eternal King,
Of wedded maid and virgin-mother born,
Our great redemption from above did bring;
For so the holy sages once did sing,
　That he our deadly forfeit should release,
And with his Father work us a perpetual peace.

That glorious form, that light insufferable,
And that far-beaming blaze of majesty,
Wherewith he wont at heaven's high council-table
To sit the midst of Trinal Unity,
He laid aside; and, here with us to be,
　Forsook the courts of everlasting day,
And chose with us a darksome house of mortal clay.

Say, heavenly Muse, shall not thy sacred vein
Afford a present to the Infant-God?
Hast thou no verse, no hymn, or solemn strain,
To welcome him to this his new abode,
Now while the heaven, by the sun's team untrod,
   Hath took no print of the approaching light,
And all the spangled host kept watch in squadron
    bright?

See, how from far, upon the eastern road,
The star-led wizards haste with odours sweet;
O run, prevent them with thy humble ode,
And lay it lowly at his blessed feet;
Have thou the honour first thy Lord to greet,
   And join thy voice unto the angel-quire,
From out his secret altar touch'd with hallow'd fire.

The Hymn.

It was the winter wild,
While the heaven-born Child
   All meanly wrapt in the rude manger lies; ·
Nature in awe to him,
Had doff'd her gaudy trim,
   With her great Master so to sympathise:
It was no season then for her
To wanton with the sun, her lusty paramour.

Only with speeches fair
She woos the gentle air
 To hide her guilty front with innocent snow ;
And on her naked shame,
Pollute with sinful blame,
 The saintly veil of maiden-white to throw ;
Confounded, that her Maker's eyes
Should look so near upon her foul deformities.

But he, her fears to cease,
Sent down the meek-eyed Peace ;
 She, crown'd with olive green, came softly sliding
Down through the turning sphere,
His ready Harbinger,
 With turtle wing the amorous clouds dividing ;
And, waving wide her myrtle wand,
She strikes an universal peace through sea and land.

No war, or battle's sound,
Was heard the world around :
 The idle spear and shield were high up-hung ;
The hooked chariot stood
Unstain'd with hostile blood ;
 The trumpet spake not to the armed throng ;
And kings sat still with awful eye,
As if they surely knew their sovran Lord was by.

But peaceful was the night
Wherein the Prince of Light
　　His reign of peace upon the earth began :
The winds with wonder whist,[1]
Smoothly the waters kist,
　　Whispering new joys to the mild ocean,
Who now hath quite forgot to rave,
While birds of calm sit brooding on the charmed wave.

The stars, with deep amaze,
Stand fix'd in steadfast gaze,
　　Bending one way their precious influence ;
And will not take their flight,
For all the morning light,
　　Or Lucifer that often warn'd them thence ;
But in their glimmering orbs did glow,
Until their Lord himself bespake, and bid them go.

And, though the shady gloom
Had given day her room,
　　The sun himself withheld his wonted speed,
And hid his head for shame,
As his inferior flame
　　The new-enlighten'd world no more should need.
He saw a greater Sun appear
Than his bright throne, or burning axletree, could bear.

---

[1] Hushed.

The shepherds on the lawn,
Or ere the point of dawn,
   Sat simply chatting in a rustic row;
Full little thought they than [1]
That the mighty Pan
   Was kindly come to live with them below;
Perhaps their loves, or else their sheep,
Was all that did their silly thoughts so busy keep.

When such music sweet
Their hearts and ears did greet,
   As never was by mortal finger strook;
Divinely-warbled voice
Answering the stringed noise,
   As all their souls in blissful rapture took:
The air such pleasure loth to lose,
With thousand echoes still prolongs each heavenly
     close.

Nature, that heard such sound,
Beneath the hollow round
   Of Cynthia's seat, the airy region thrilling,
Now was almost won
To think her part was done,
   And that her reign had here its last fulfilling;

---

[1] Old form of *then.*

She knew such harmony alone
Could hold all heaven and earth in happier union.

At last surrounds their sight
A globe of circular light,
    That with long beams the shamefaced night array'd ;
The helmed cherubim,
And sworded seraphim,
    Are seen in glittering ranks with wings display'd,
Harping in loud and solemn quire,
With unexpressive notes, to Heaven's new-born Heir.

Such music (as 'tis said)
Before was never made,
    But when of old the sons of morning sung,
While the Creator great
His constellations set,
    And the well-balanced world on hinges hung ;
And cast the dark foundations deep,
And bid the weltering waves their oozy channel keep.

Ring out, ye crystal spheres,
Once bless our human ears,
    If ye have power to touch our senses so ;

And let your silver chime
Move in melodious time ;
   And let the base of Heaven's deep organ blow ;
And, with your ninefold harmony,
Make up full consort to the angelic symphony.

For, if such holy song,
Enwrap our fancy long,
   Time will run back and fetch the age of gold ;
And speckled Vanity
Will sicken soon and die,
   And leprous Sin will melt from earthly mould ;
And Hell itself will pass away,
And leave her dolorous mansions to the peering
     day.

Yea, Truth and Justice then
Will down return to men.
   Orb'd in a rainbow ; and, like glories wearing,
Mercy will sit between,
Throned in celestial sheen,
   With radiant feet the tissued clouds down steering ;
And Heaven, as at some festival,
Will open wide the gates of her high palace-hall.

G

But wisest Fate says No,
This must not yet be so,
   The Babe yet lies in smiling infancy,
That on the bitter cross
Must redeem our loss ;
   So both himself and us to glorify :
Yet first, to those ychain'd in sleep,
The wakeful trump of doom must thunder through the
     deep ;

With such a horrid clang
As on Mount Sinai rang,
   While the red fire and smouldering clouds outbrake :
The aged earth aghast
With terror of that blast,
   Shall from the surface to the centre shake ;
When at the world's last session,
The dreadful Judge in middle air shall spread his
     throne.

And then at last our bliss
Full and perfect is,
   But now begins ; for, from this happy day,
The Old Dragon, under ground
In straiter limits bound,
   Not half so far casts his usurped sway ;

And, wroth to see his kingdom fail,
Swinges the scaly horror of his folded tail.

The oracles are dumb,
No voice or hideous hum
   Runs through the arched roof in words deceiving.
Apollo from his shrine
Can no more divine,
   With hollow shriek the steep of Delphos leaving.
No nightly trance, or breathed spell,
Inspires the pale-eyed priest from the prophetic cell.

The lonely mountains o'er,
And the resounding shore,
   A voice of weeping heard and loud lament ;
From haunted spring and dale,
Edged with poplar pale,
   The parting Genius is with sighing sent ;
With flower-inwoven tresses torn,
The Nymphs in twilight shade of tangled thickets
     mourn.

In consecrated earth,
And on the holy hearth
   The Lars, and Lemures, moan with midnight plaint ;

In urns, and altars round,
A drear and dying sound
   Affrights the Flamens at their service quaint;
And the chill marble seems to sweat,
While each peculiar power foregoes his wonted seat.

Peor and Baälim
Forsake their temples dim
   With that twice-batter'd god of Palestine;
And mooned Ashtaroth,
Heaven's queen and mother both,
   Now sits not girt with tapers' holy shrine;
The Libyc Hammon shrinks his horn,
In vain the Tyrian maids their wounded Thammuz
      mourn.

And sullen Moloch, fled,
Hath left in shadows dread
   His burning idol all of blackest hue;
In vain with cymbals' ring
They call the grisly king,
   In dismal dance about the furnace blue;
The brutish gods of Nile as fast,
Isis, and Orus, and the dog Anubis, haste.

Nor is Osiris seen
In Memphian grove or green,
   Trampling the unshower'd grass with lowings loud :
Nor can he be at rest
Within his sacred chest ;
   Nought but profoundest hell can be his shroud ;
In vain with timbrell'd anthems dark
The sable-stoled sorcerers bear his worshipt ark.

He feels from Judah's land
The dreaded Infant's hand,
   The rays of Bethlehem blind his dusky eyn ;
Nor all the gods beside
Longer dare abide,
   Nor Typhon huge ending in snaky twine :
Our Babe, to show his Godhead true,
Can in his swaddling bands control the damned crew.

So, when the sun in bed,
Curtain'd with cloudy red,
   Pillows his chin upon an orient wave,
The flocking shadows pale
Troop to the infernal jail,
   Each fetter'd ghost slips to his several grave ;

And the yellow-skirted fays
Fly after the night-steeds, leaving their moon-loved
maze.

But see, the Virgin blest
Hath laid her Babe to rest ;
Time is our tedious song should here have ending :
Heaven's youngest-teemed star
Hath fix'd her polish'd car,
Her sleeping Lord, with handmaid-lamp attending :
And all about the courtly stable
Bright-harness'd[1] angels sit in order serviceable.

[1] In bright armour.

By Giles Fletcher.

Who can forget—never to be forgot.

WHO can forget—never to be forgot—
    The time, that all the world in slumber lies,
When, like the stars, the singing angels shot
To earth, and heaven awaked all his eyes,
To see another sun at midnight rise
    On earth ? Was never sight of pareil [1] fame
    For God before, man like himself did frame,
But God himself now like a mortal man became.

A Child he was, and had not learnt to speak,
That with his word the world before did make ;
His mother's arms him bore, he was so weak,
That with one hand the vaults of heaven could shake ;
See how small room my infant Lord doth take
    Whom all the world is not enough to hold !
    Who of his years, or of his age hath told?
Never such age so young, never a child so old.

---

[1] Equal.

And yet but newly he was infanted,
And yet already he was sought to die;
Yet scarcely born, already banished;
Not able yet to go, and forced to fly:
But scarcely fled away, when by and by,
    The tyran's [1] sword with blood is all defiled,
    And Rachel, for her sons, with fury wild,
Cries, "O thou cruel king, and O my sweetest
    Child!"

Egypt his nurse became, where Nilus springs,
Who, straight to entertain the rising sun,
The hasty harvest in his bosom brings;
But now for drought the fields were all undone,
And now with waters all is overrun:
    So fast the Cynthian mountains pour'd their
        snow,
    When once they felt the sun so near them
        glow,
That Nilus Egypt lost, and to a sea did grow.

The angels carolled loud their song of peace;
The cursed oracles were strucken dumb;
To see their Shepherd, the poor shepherds press;

---

[1] *Tyran* is the old form of *Tyrant.*

To see their King, the kingly sophies [1] come ;
And them to guide unto his Master's home,
    A star comes dancing up the Orient,
    That springs for joy over the strawy tent,
Where gold, to make their prince a crown, they all
    present.

---

[1] Wise men.

*From Henry Vaughan's Silex
Scintillans.*

The Shepherds.

SWEET, harmless livers! on whose holy leisure
    Waits innocence and pleasure;
Whose leaders to those pastures and clear springs
    Were patriarchs, saints and kings;
How happened it that in the dead of night
    You only saw true light,
While Palestine was fast asleep and lay
    Without one thought of day?
Was it because those first and blessèd swains
    Were pilgrims on those plains
When they received the promise, for which now
    'Twas there first shown to you?
'Tis true he loves that dust whereon they go
    That serve him here below,
And therefore might for memory of those
    His love there first disclose;
But wretched Salem, once his love, must now
    No voice nor vision know;

Her stately piles with all their height and pride
    Now languishèd and died,
And Bethlem's humble cots above them stept
    While all her seers slept ;
Her cedar fir, hewed stones, and gold were all
    Polluted through their fall ;
And those once sacred mansions were now
    Mere emptiness and show.
This made the angel call at reeds and thatch,
    Yet where the shepherds watch,
And God's own lodging, though he could not lack,
    To be a common rack.
No costly pride, no soft-clothed luxury
    In those thin cells could lie ;
Each stirring wind and storm blew through their cots,
    Which never harboured plots ;
Only content and love and humble joys
    Lived there without all noise ;
Perhaps some harmless cares for the next day
    Did in their bosoms play,
As where to lead their sheep, what silent nook,
    What springs or shades to look ;
But that was all ; and now with gladsome care
    They for the town prepare ;
They leave their flock, and in a busy talk
    All towards Bethlem walk,

To seek their soul's great Shepherd who was come
  To bring all stragglers home ;
Where now they find him out, and, taught before,
  That Lamb of God adore,
That Lamb, whose days great kings and prophets
    wished
  And longed to see, but missed.
The first light they beheld was bright and gay,
  And turned their night to day ;
But to this later light they saw in him
  Their day was dark and dim.

From Henry Vaughan's Silex Scintillans.

Christ's Nativity.

AWAKE, glad heart! get up and sing!
    It is the Birthday of thy King.
        Awake! awake!
        The sun doth shake
Light from his locks, and, all the way
Breathing perfumes, doth spice the day.

2.

Awake! awake! hark how th' wood rings,
Winds whisper, and the busy springs
        A concert make!
        Awake! awake!
Man is their high-priest, and should rise
To offer up the sacrifice.

3.

I would I were some bird, or star,
Fluttering in woods, or lifted far
            Above this inn,
            And road of sin!
Then either star or bird should be
Shining or singing still to thee.

4.

I would I had in my best part
Fit rooms for thee! or that my heart
            Were so clean as
            Thy manger was!
But I am all filth, and obscene;
Yet, if thou wilt, thou canst make clean.

5.

Sweet Jesu! will then.   Let no more
This leper haunt and soil thy door!
            Cure him, ease him,
            O release him!
And let once more, by mystic birth,
The Lord of life be born in earth.

By Robert Southwell.

Rew Prince, Rew Pomp.

BEHOLD a silly tender Babe,
   In freezing winter night,
In homely manger trembling lies;
   Alas! a piteous sight.

The inns are full, no man will yield
   This little pilgrim bed;
But forced he is with silly beasts
   In crib to shroud his head.

Despise him not for lying there,
   First what he is inquire;
An orient pearl is often found
   In depth of dirty mire.

Weigh not his crib, his wooden dish,
   Nor beast that by him feed;
Weigh not his mother's poor attire,
   Nor Joseph's simple weed.[1]

---

[1] Dress.

This stable is a prince's court,
    This crib his chair of state ;
The beasts are parcel of his pomp,
    The wooden dish his plate.

The persons in that poor attire
    His royal liveries wear ;
The Prince himself is come from heaven,
    This pomp is praisèd there.

With joy approach, O Christian wight !
    Do homage to thy King ;
And highly praise this humble pomp
    Which he from heaven doth bring.

From George Herbert's Temple.

Christmas.

ALL after pleasures as I rid one day,
　　My horse and I both tired, body and mind,
　With full cry of affections quite astray,
I took up in the next inn I could find.

There, when I came, whom found I but my dear—
　My dearest Lord; expecting till the grief
　Of pleasures brought me to him; ready there
To be all passengers' most sweet relief?

O thou, whose glorious, yet contracted, light,
　Wrapt in night's mantle, stole into a manger;
　Since my dark soul and brutish is thy right,
To man, of all beasts be not thou a stranger;

Furnish and deck my soul, that thou may'st have
A better lodging than a rack or grave.

H

The shepherds sing ; and shall I silent be ?
    My God, no hymn for thee ?
My soul's a shepherd too ; a flock it feeds
    Of thoughts and words and deeds.
The pasture is thy word, the streams thy grace,
    Enriching every place.

Shepherd and flock shall sing, and all my powers
    Outsing the daylight hours.
Then we will chide the sun for letting night
    Take up his place and right :
We sing one common Lord ; wherefore he should
    Himself the candle hold.

I will go searching till I find a sun
    Shall stay till we have done ;
A willing shiner, that shall shine as gladly
    As frost-nipt suns look sadly.
Then we will sing and shine all our own day,
    And one another pay.

His beams shall cheer my breast ; and both so twine,
Till ev'n his beams sing and my music shine.

By Bishop Hall.

For Christmas Day.

IMMORTAL Babe, who this dear day
  Didst change thine heaven for our clay,
And didst with flesh thy godhead veil,
Eternal Son of God, all hail !

Shine, happy star ; ye angels, sing
Glory on high to heaven's King :
Run, shepherds, leave your nightly watch,
See heaven come down to Bethlehem's cratch.

Worship, ye sages of the east,
The King of gods in meanness dressed.
O blessed maid, smile and adore
The God thy womb and arms have bore.

Star, angels, shepherds, and wise sages,
Thou virgin glory of all ages,
Restored frame of heaven and earth,
Joy in your dear Redeemer's birth !

By Edmund Bolton. From England's Helicon, 1600.

The Shepherd's Song.

A CAROL OR HYMN FOR CHRISTMAS.

SWEET music, sweeter far
    Than any song is sweet:
Sweet music, heavenly rare,
    Mine ears, O peers, doth greet.
You gentle flocks, whose fleeces, pearled with dew,
    Resemble heaven, whom golden drops make bright,
Listen, O listen, now, O not to you
    Our pipes make sport to shorten weary night:
        But voices most divine
        Make blissful harmony:
        Voices that seem to shine,
        For what else clears the sky?
Tunes can we hear, but not the singers see,
The tunes divine, and so the singers be.

        Lo, how the firmament
        Within an azure fold
        The flock of stars hath pent,
        That we might them behold

Yet from their beams proceedeth not this light,
  Nor can their christals such reflection give.
What then doth make the element so bright?
  The heavens are come down upon earth to live.
    But hearken to the song,
      Glory to glory's king,
    And peace all men among,
      These quiristers do sing.
Angels they are, as also (Shepherds) he
Whom in our fear we do admire to see.

    Let not amazement blind
      Your souls, said he, annoy:
    To you and all mankind
      My message bringeth joy.
For lo, the world's great Shepherd now is born,
  A blessed babe, an infant full of power:
After long night uprisen is the morn,
  Renowning Bethl'em in the Saviour.
    Sprung is the perfect day,
      By prophets seen afar:
    Sprung is the mirthful May,
      Which winter cannot mar.
In David's city doth this sun appear
Clouded in flesh, yet, shepherds, sit we here?

By Ben Jonson.

A Hymn on the Nativity of my Saviour.

I SING the birth was born to-night,
    The author both of life and light;
The angels so did sound it.
And like the ravished shepherds said,
Who saw the light, and were afraid,
    Yet searched, and true they found it.

The Son of God, th' eternal king,
That did us all salvation bring,
    And freed the soul from danger;
He whom the whole world could not take,
The Word, which heaven and earth did make,
    Was now laid in a manger.

The Father's wisdom willed it so,
The Son's obedience knew no No,
    Both wills were in one stature;
And as that wisdom had decreed,
The Word was now made flesh indeed,
    And took on him our nature.

What comfort by him do we win,
Who made himself the price of sin,
  To make us heirs of glory !
To see this babe all innocence ;
A martyr born in our defence :
  Can man forget the story ?

*From Richard Crashaw's Steps to the
Temple. The text of ed. 1648 is followed.*

A Hymn of the Nativity.

SUNG AS BY THE SHEPHERDS.

Chorus.　COME we shepherds whose blest sight
　　　　Hath met Love's noon in Nature's night;
　　Come, lift we up our loftier song,
　　And wake the sun that lies too long.

　　To all our world of well-stol'n joy,
　　　He slept and dreamt of no such thing,
　　While we found out heaven's fairer eye
　　　And kist the cradle of our King;
　　Tell him he rises now too late
　　To show us ought worth looking at.

　　Tell him we now can show him more
　　　Than e'er he showed to mortal sight,
　　Than he himself e'er saw before,
　　　Which to be seen needs not his light.
　　Tell him, Tityrus, where th' hast been,
　　Tell him, Thyrsis, what th' hast seen.

Tit. Gloomy night embraced the place
      Where the noble Infant lay,
The Babe looked up and showed his face;
      In spite of darkness it was day.
It was thy day, Sweet, and did rise
Not from the East but from thine eyes.
      Chorus. It was thy day, Sweet, &c.

Thyrs. Winter chid aloud and sent
      The angry North to wage his wars;
The North forgot his fierce intent,
      And left perfumes instead of scars;
By those sweet eyes' persuasive powers,
Where he meant frost he scattered flowers.
      Chorus. By those sweet eyes, &c.

Both. We saw thee in thy balmy nest,
      Bright dawn of our eternal day!
We saw thine eyes break from their East
      And chase the trembling shades away;
We saw thee, and we blest the sight,
We saw thee by thine own sweet light.

Tit. Poor world (said I), what wilt thou do
      To entertain this starry stranger?
Is this the best thou canst bestow,
      A cold and not too cleanly manger?

Contend, ye powers of heaven and earth,
To fit a bed for this huge birth.
   Chorus. Contend, ye powers, &c.

Thyrs. Proud world (said I), cease your contest,
  And let the mighty Babe alone,
The Phœnix builds the Phœnix nest,
  Love's architecture is all one.
The Babe whose birth embraves this morn
Made his own bed ere he was born.
   Chorus. The Babe whose birth, &c.

'Tit. I saw the curl'd drops, soft and slow,
  Come hovering o'er the place's head,
Offering their whitest sheets of snow
  To furnish the fair Infant's bed :
Forbear (said I), be not too bold ;
Your fleece is white, but 'tis too cold.
   Chorus. Forbear (said I), &c.

Thyrs. I saw the obsequious seraphins
  Their rosy fleece of fire bestow ;
For well they now can spare their wings,
  Since heaven itself lies here below :
Well done (said I), but are you sure
Your down so warm will pass for pure.
   Chorus. Well done (said I), &c.

Tit. No, no, your king's not yet to seek
    Where to repose his royal head,
See, see, how soon his new-bloom'd cheek
    Twixt 's mother's breasts is gone to bed :
Sweet choice (said I), no way but so,
Not to lie cold, yet sleep in snow.
    Chorus. Sweet choice (said I), &c.

Both. We saw thee in thy balmy nest,
    Bright dawn of our eternal day !
We saw thine eyes break from their East
    And chase the trembling shades away ;
We saw thee, and we blest the sight,
We saw thee by thine own sweet light.
    Chorus. We saw thee, &c.

Full Chorus. Welcome all wonder in one sight,
    Eternity shut in a span,
Summer in winter, day in night,
    Heaven in earth and God in man !
Great little One ! whose all-embracing birth
Lifts earth to heaven, stoops heaven to earth.

Welcome, though not to gold nor silk,
    To more than Cæsar's birthright is,
Two Sister Seas of Virgin milk
    With many a rarely-tempered kiss,

That breathes at once both Maid and Mother,
Warms in the one and cools in the other.

She sings thy tears asleep, and dips
    Her kisses in thy weeping eye ;
She spreads the red leaves of thy lips
    That in their buds yet blushing lie :
She 'gainst those mother-diamonds tries
The points of her young eagle's eyes.

Welcome, though not to those gay flies
    Gilded i' the beams of earthly kings,
Slippery souls in smiling eyes,
    But to poor shepherds' home-spun things ;
Whose wealth's their flock, whose wit to be
Well read in their simplicity.

Yet when young April's husband-showers
    Shall bless the fruitful Maia's bed,
We'll bring the first-born of her flowers
    To kiss thy feet and crown thy head :
To thee, dread Lamb, whose love must keep
The shepherds more than they their sheep.

To thee, meek Majesty ! soft King
 Of simple graces and sweet loves,
Each of us his lamb will bring,
 Each his pair of silver doves,
Till burnt at last in fire of thy fair eyes
Ourselves become our own best sacrifice.

From Richard Crashaw's Steps to the Temple. Only the opening lines are here given.

A hymn for the Epiphany.

SUNG AS BY THE THREE KINGS.

1 *King.* BRIGHT Babe! whose awful beauties make
        The morn incur a sweet mistake;

2 *King.* For whom the officious heavens devise
        To disinherit the sun's rise;

3 *King.* Delicately to displace
        The day, and plant it fairer in thy face;

1 *King.* O thou born King of loves!

2 *King.* Of lights!

3 *King.* Of joys!

Chorus. Look up, sweet Babe, look up and see!
        For love of thee,
        Thus far from home
        The East is come
        To seek herself in thy sweet eyes.

1 *King.* We who strangely went astray,
        Lost in a bright
        Meridian night;

2 *King.* A darkness made of too much day;

3 *King.* Beckoned from far
By thy fair star,
Lo, at last have found our way.

Chorus. To thee, thou Day of Night! thou East of
West !
Lo, we at last have found the way
To thee, the world's great universal East,
The general and indifferent day.

1 *King.* All-circling point! all-centring sphere !
The world's one round eternal year:

2 *King.* Whose full and all-unwrinkled face
Nor sinks nor swells with time or place ;

3 *King.* But every where and every while
Is one consistent solid smile.

1 *King.* Not vexed and tost,

2 *King.* 'Twixt spring and frost ;

3 *King.* Nor by alternate shreds of light,
Sordidly shifting hands with shades and night.

Chorus. O little All, in Thy embrace,
The world lies warm and likes his place ;
Nor does his full globe fail to be
Kissed on both his cheeks by Thee ;
Time is too narrow for Thy year,
Nor makes the whole world Thy half-sphere.

*By William Drummond
of Hawthornden.*

The Angels.

RUN, shepherds, run where Bethlehem blest
  appears.
 We bring the best of news; be not dismayed;
A Saviour there is born more old than years,
 Amidst heaven's rolling height this earth who stayed.
 In a poor cottage inned, a virgin maid
A weakling did him bear, who all upbears;
 There is he poorly swaddled, in manger laid,
To whom too narrow swaddlings are our spheres:
Run, shepherds, run and solemnise his birth.
 This is that night—no, day, grown great with bliss,
 In which the power of Satan broken is:
In Heaven be glory, peace unto the earth!
 Thus singing, through the air the angels swam,
 And cope of stars re-echoèd the same.

*By William Drummond
of Hawthornden.*

The Shepherds.

O THAN the fairest day, thrice fairer night!
   Night to blest days in which a sun doth rise
  Of which that golden eye which clears the skies
Is but a sparkling ray, a shadow-light!
And blessed ye, in silly pastors' sight,
   Mild creatures, in whose warm crib now lies
That heaven-sent youngling, holy-maid-born wight,
   Midst, end, beginning of our prophecies!
Blest cottage that hath flowers in winter spread,
   Though withered—blessed grass that hath the grace
  To deck and be a carpet to that place!
Thus sang, unto the sounds of oaten reed,
   Before the Babe, the shepherds bowed on knees;
   And springs ran nectar, honey dropped from trees.

I

By Sir John Beaumont.

Of the Epiphany.

FAIR eastern star, that art ordained to run
    Before the sages, to the rising sun,
Here cease thy course, and wonder that the cloud
Of this poor stable can thy Maker shroud :
Ye heavenly bodies glory to be bright,
And are esteemed as ye are rich in light ;
But here on earth is taught a different way,
Since under this low roof the Highest lay.
Jerusalem erects her stately towers,
Displays her windows and adorns her bowers ;
Yet there thou must not cast a trembling spark,
Let Herod's palace still continue dark ;
Each school and synagogue thy force repels,
There Pride enthroned in misty error dwells ;
The temple, where the priests maintain their quire,
Shall taste no beam of thy celestial fire,
While this weak cottage all thy splendour takes :
A joyful gate of every chink it makes.

Here shines no golden roof, no ivory stair,
No king exalted in a stately chair,
Girt with attendants, or by heralds styled,
But straw and hay enwrap a speechless child.
Yet Sabae's lords before this babe unfold
Their treasures, offering incense, myrrh and gold.
The crib becomes an altar: therefore dies
No ox nor sheep; for in their fodder lies
The Prince of Peace, who, thankful for his bed,
Destroys those rites in which their blood was shed :
The quintessence of earth he takes, and fees,
And precious gums distilled from weeping trees;
Rich metals and sweet odours now declare
The glorious blessings which his laws prepare,
To clear us from the base and loathsome flood
Of sense and make us fit for angels' food,
Who lift to God for us the holy smoke
Of fervent prayers with which we him invoke,
And try our actions in the searching fire
By which the seraphims our lips inspire :
No muddy dross pure minerals shall infect,
We shall exhale our vapours up direct :
No storm shall cross, nor glittering lights deface
Perpetual sighs which seek a happy place.

*From Jeremy Taylor's Festival
Hymns.*

ibymn for Cbristmas=Day.

BEING À DIALOGUE BETWEEN THREE SHEPHERDS.

1. WHERE is this blessed Babe
            That hath made
All the world so full of joy
            And expectation ;
            That glorious boy
            That crowns each nation
With a triumphant wreath of blessedness?

2. Where should he be but in the throng,
            And among
His angel ministers, that sing
            And take wing
Just as may echo to his voice,
            And rejoice,
When wing and tongue and all
May so procure their happiness?

3. But he hath other waiters now :
A poor cow,
An ox and mule, stand and behold,
And wonder
That a stable should enfold
Him that can thunder.

Chorus. O what a gracious God have we,
How good ! how great ! even as our misery.

From Jeremy Taylor's Festival Hymns.

A Hymn for Christmas Day.

AWAKE, my soul, and come away :
    Put on thy best array ;
    Lest if thou longer stay
Thou lose some minutes of so blest a day.
                Go run
And bid good-morrow to the sun ;
Welcome his safe return
          To Capricorn,
    And that great morn
    Wherein a God was born,
    Whose story none can tell
But he whose every word's a miracle.

To-day Almightiness grew weak ;
The Word itself was mute and could not speak.

That Jacob's star which made the sun
To dazzle if he durst look on,
Now mantled o'er in Bethlehem's night,
Borrowed a star to show him light.

He that begirt each zone,
To whom both poles are one,
Who grasped the Zodiac in his hand
And made it move or stand,
Is now by nature man,
By stature but a span ;
Eternity is now grown short ;
A King is born without a court ;
The water thirsts ; the fountain's dry ;
And life, being born, made apt to die.

Chorus. Then let our praises emulate and vie
   With his humility !
  Since he's exiled from skies
   That we might rise,—
  From low estate of men
  Let's sing him up again !
  Each man wind up his heart
  To bear a part
In that angelic choir and show
  His glory high as he was low.
Let's sing towards men goodwill and charity,
 Peace upon earth, glory to God on high !
    Hallelujah ! Hallelujah !

By Sir Edward Sherburne.

And they laid Him in a Manger.

HAPPY crib, that wert alone
    To my God, bed, cradle, throne !
Whilst thy glorious vileness I
View with divine fancy's eye,
Sordid filth seems all the cost,
State, and splendour, crowns do boast.

See heaven's sacred majesty
Humbled beneath poverty ;
Swaddled up in homely rags
On a bed of straw and flags !
He whose hands the heavens displayed,
And the world's foundations laid,
From the world's almost exiled,
Of all ornaments despoiled.
Perfumes bathe him not, new-born,
Persian mantles not adorn ;
Nor do the rich roofs look bright
With the jasper's orient light.

Where, O royal Infant, be
Th' ensigns of thy majesty;
Thy Sire's equalizing state;
And thy sceptre that rules fate?
Where's thy angel-guarded throne,
Whence thy laws thou didst make known—
Laws which heaven, earth, hell obeyed?
These, ah! these aside he laid;
Would the emblem be—of pride
By humility outvied?

By Robert Herrick.

An Ode on the Birth of our Saviour.

IN numbers, and but these few,
　　I sing thy birth, O Jesu!
Thou pretty baby, born here
With sup'rabundant scorn here:
Who for thy princely port here,
　　　　Hadst for thy place
　　　　Of birth, a base
Out-stable for thy court here.

Instead of neat enclosures
Of interwoven osiers,
Instead of fragrant posies
Of daffodills and roses,
Thy cradle, kingly stranger,
　　　　As gospel tells,
　　　　Was nothing else
But here a homely manger.

But we with silks not crewels,
With sundry precious jewels,
And lily work will dress thee ;
And, as we dispossess thee
Of clouts, we'll make a chamber,
      Sweet babe, for thee
      Of ivory,
And plaster'd round with amber.

The Jews they did disdain thee,
But we will entertain thee
With glories to await here
 Upon thy princely state here ;
And, more for love than pity,
      From year to year
      We'll make thee here
A free-born of our city.

By Francis Kinwelmersh. From the
Paradise of Dayntie Deuises, 1576.

For Christmas Day.

REJOICE, rejoice, with heart and voice !
    In Christè's birth this day rejoice !
From Virgin's womb this day did spring
The precious seed that only saved man ;
This day let man rejoice and sweetly sing,
Since on this day salvation first began.
    This day did Christ man's soul from death remove,
    With glorious saints to dwell in heaven above.

This day to man came pledge of perfect peace,
This day to man came perfect unity,
This day man's grief began for to surcease,
This day did man receive a remedy
    For each offence and every deadly sin
    With guilty heart that erst he wandered in.

In Christè's flock let love be surely placed,
From Christè's flock let concord hate expel,
Of Christè's flock let love be so embraced
As we in Christ and Christ in us may dwell;
    Christ is the author of all unity,
    From whence proceedeth all felicity.

O sing unto this glittering glorious king,
O praise his name let every living thing,
Let heart and voice, like bells of silver, ring
The comfort that this day doth bring.
    Let lute, let shawm, with sound of sweet delight,
    The joy of Christè's birth this day recite.

By S. T. Coleridge.

The Virgin's Cradle-Hymn.[1]

DORMI, Jesu ! Mater ridet
    Quae tam dulcem somnum videt,
Dormi, Jesu ! blandule !
Si non dormis, Mater plorat
Inter fila cantans orat,
    Blande, veni, somnule.

English.

Sleep, sweet babe ! my cares beguiling :
Mother sits beside thee smiling ;
    Sleep, my darling, tenderly !
If thou sleep not, mother mourneth,
Singing as her wheel she turneth :
    Come, soft slumber, balmily !

---

[1] Copied from a print of the Virgin in a Roman Catholic village in Germany.

By John Addington Symonds.

A Christmas Lullaby.

SLEEP, baby, sleep!   The Mother sings:
 Heaven's angels kneel and fold their wings:
  Sleep, baby, sleep!

With swathes of scented hay thy bed
By Mary's hand at eve was spread.
  Sleep, baby, sleep!

At midnight came the shepherds, they
Whom seraphs wakened by the way.
  Sleep, baby, sleep!

And three kings from the East afar
Ere dawn came guided by thy star.
  Sleep, baby, sleep!

They brought thee gifts of gold and gems,
Pure orient pearls, rich diadems.
  Sleep, baby, sleep!

But thou who liest slumbering there,
Art King of kings, earth, ocean, air.
Sleep, baby, sleep !

Sleep, baby, sleep !   The shepherds sing :
Through heaven, through earth, hosannas ring.
Sleep, baby, sleep !

*From George Wither's Hallelujah,
or Britain's Second Remem-
brancer.*

A Rocking Hymn.

SWEET baby, sleep; what ails my dear?
　　What ails my darling thus to cry?
Be still, my child, and lend thine ear
　　To hear me sing thy lullaby.
　　　　My pretty lamb, forbear to weep;
　　　　Be still, my dear; sweet baby, sleep.

Thou blessed soul, what canst thou fear?
　　What thing to thee can mischief do?
Thy God is now thy Father dear;
　　His holy Spouse thy Mother too.
　　　　Sweet baby, then, forbear to weep;
　　　　Be still, my babe; sweet baby, sleep.

　　·　·　·　·　·　·　·　　·

Whilst thus thy lullaby I sing,
　　For thee great blessings ripening be;

K

Thine eldest brother is a king,
  And hath a kingdom bought for thee.
      Sweet baby, then, forbear to weep ;
      Be still, my babe ; sweet baby, sleep.

Sweet baby, sleep, and nothing fear,
  For whosoever thee offends,
By thy protector threatened are,
  And God and angels are thy friends.
      Sweet baby, then, forbear to weep ;
      Be still, my babe ; sweet baby, sleep.

When God with us was dwelling here,
  In little babes he took delight :
Such innocents as thou, my dear,
  Are ever precious in his sight.
      Sweet baby, then, forbear to weep ;
      Be still, my babe ; sweet baby, sleep.

A little infant once was he,
  And Strength-in-Weakness then was laid
Upon his Virgin-Mother's knee,
  That power to thee might be conveyed.
      Sweet baby, then, forbear to weep ;
      Be still, my babe ; sweet baby, sleep.

In this thy frailty and thy need
   He friends and helpers doth prepare,
Which thee shall cherish, clothe, and feed,
   For of thy weal they tender are.
      Sweet baby, then, forbear to weep ;
      Be still, my babe ; sweet baby, sleep.

The King of kings, when he was born,
   Had not so much for outward ease ;
By him such dressings were not worn,
   Nor such-like swaddling-clothes as these.
      Sweet baby, then, forbear to weep ;
      Be still, my babe ; sweet baby, sleep.

Within a manger lodged thy Lord,
   Where oxen lay and asses fed ;
Warm rooms we do to thee afford,
   An easy cradle or a bed.
      Sweet baby, then, forbear to weep ;
      Be still, my babe ; sweet baby, sleep.

The wants that he did then sustain
   Have purchased wealth, my babe, for thee,
And by his torments and his pain
   Thy rest and ease secured be.
      My baby, then, forbear to weep ;
      Be still, my babe ; sweet baby, sleep.

Thou hast (yet more), to perfect this,
   A promise and an earnest got
Of gaining everlasting bliss,
   Though thou, my babe, perceiv'st it not.
       Sweet baby, then, forbear to weep;
       Be still, my babe; sweet baby, sleep.

PART III.

CHRISTMAS CUSTOMS AND CHRISTMAS CHEER.

From George Wither's Juvenilia.

So, now is come our joyfulst feast.

SO, now is come our joyfulst feast,
    Let every man be jolly;
Each room with ivy leaves is drest,
    And every post with holly.
Though some churls at our mirth repine,
Round your foreheads garlands twine;
Drown sorrow in a cup of wine,
    And let us all be merry.

Now all our neighbours' chimnies smoke,
    And Christmas logs are burning;
Their ovens they with baked meats choke,
    And all their spits are turning.

Without the door let sorrow lie;
And if for cold it hap to die,
We'll bury't in a Christmas pie,
　　And evermore be merry.

Now every lad is wondrous trim,
　　And no man minds his labour;
Our lasses have provided them
　　A bag-pipe and a tabor;
Young men and maids, and girls and boys,
Give life to one another's joys;
And you anon shall by their noise
　　Perceive that they are merry.

Rank misers now do sparing shun;
　　Their hall of music soundeth;
And dogs thence with whole shoulders run,
　　So all things there aboundeth.
The country folks themselves advance
For crowdy-mutton's [1] come out of France;
And Jack shall pipe, and Jill shall dance,
　　And all the town be merry.

Ned Squash hath fetched his bands from pawn,
　　And all his best apparel;
Brisk Ned hath bought a ruff of lawn
　　With droppings of the barrel;

---

[1] Fiddlers.

And those that hardly all the year
Had bread to eat or rags to wear
Will have both clothes and dainty fare,
    And all the day be merry.

Now poor men to the justices
    With capons make their arrants;
And if they hap to fail of these,
    They plague them with their warrants:
But now they feed them with good cheer,
And what they want they take in beer;
For Christmas comes but once a year,
    And then they shall be merry.

Good farmers in the country nurse
    The poor that else were undone;
Some landlords spend their money worse
    On lust and pride at London.
There the roysters they do play,
Drab and dice their lands away,
Which may be ours another day;
    And therefore let's be merry.

The client now his suit forbears,
    The prisoner's heart is eased;
The debtor drinks away his cares,
    And for the time is pleased.

Though other purses be more fat,
Why should we pine or grieve at that?
Hang sorrow! care will kill a cat,
   And therefore let's be merry.

Hark! how the wags abroad do call
   Each other forth to rambling:
Anon you'll see them in the hall
   For nuts and apples scrambling.
Hark! how the roofs with laughter sound!
Anon they'll think the house goes round:
For they the cellar's depth have found,
   And there they will be merry.

The wenches with their wassail bowls
   About the streets are singing;
The boys are come to catch the owls,
   The wild mare in is bringing.
Our kitchen-boy hath broke his box,
And to the dealing of the ox
Our honest neighbours come by flocks,
   And here they will be merry.

Now kings and queens poor sheep-cotes have
   And mate with everybody;
The honest now may play the knave
   And wise men play at noddy.

Some youths will now a mumming go,
Some others play at Rowland-ho,
And twenty other gameboys mo,
　Because they will be merry.

Then wherefore in these merry days,
　Should we, I pray, be duller?
No, let us sing some roundelays
　To make our mirth the fuller.
And whilst thus inspir'd we sing,
Let all the streets with echoes ring,
Woods and hills and everything
　Bear witness we are merry.

By Robert Herrick.

Ceremonies for Christmas.

COME, bring with a noise,
　My merry, merry boys,
The Christmas log to the firing ;
　While my good dame, she
　Bids ye all be free ;
And drink to your heart's desiring

　With the last year's brand
　Light the new block, and
For good success in his spending,
　On your psaltries play,
　That sweet luck may
Come while the log is a teending.[1]

　Drink now the strong beer,
　Cut the white loaf here,
The while the meat is a shredding ;
　For the rare mince-pie
　And the plums stand by
To fill the paste that's a kneading.

---

[1] Burning.

CHRISTMAS EVE; ANOTHER CEREMONY.

Come, guard this night the Christmas-pie,
That the thief, though ne'er so sly,
With his flesh hooks don't come nigh
           To catch it,

From him, who all alone sits there,
Having his eyes still in his ear,
And a deal of nightly fear
           To watch it.

———

ANOTHER TO THE MAIDS.

Wash your hands, or else the fire
Will not teend to your desire;
Unwashed hands, ye maidens know,
Dead the fire, though ye blow.

———

ANOTHER.

WASSAIL the trees that they may bear
You many a plum, and many a pear:
For more or less fruits they will bring,
As you do give them wassailing.

*There is a black letter copy of this song
in the Pepysian Collection. The
first part is found in Durfey's Pills
to Purge Melancholy. I have followed the text given in Rimbault's
Little Book of Songs and Ballads.*

The Praise of Christmas.

FIRST PART.

ALL hail to the days that merit more praise
    Than all the rest of the year,
And welcome the nights that double delights
    As well for the poor as the peer !
Good fortune attend each merry man's friend,
    That doth but the best that he may ;
Forgetting old wrongs, with carols and songs,
    To drive the cold winter away.

Let Misery pack, with a whip at his back,
    To the deep Tantalian flood ;
In Lethe profound let envy be drown'd,
    That pines at another man's good ;
Let Sorrow's expense be banded from hence,
    All payments have greater delay,
We'll spend the long nights in cheerful delights
    To drive the cold winter away.

'Tis ill for a mind to anger inclined
 To think of small injuries now;
If wrath be to seek do not lend her thy cheek,
 Nor let her inhabit thy brow.
Cross out of thy books malevolent looks,
 Both beauty and youth's decay,
And wholly consort with mirth and with sport
 To drive the cold winter away.

The court in all state now opens her gate
 And gives a free welcome to most;
The city likewise, tho' somewhat precise,
 Doth willingly part with her roast:
But yet by report from city and court
 The country will e'er gain the day;
More liquor is spent and with better content
 To drive the cold winter away.

Our good gentry there for costs do not spare,
 The yeomanry fast not till Lent;
The farmers and such think nothing too much,
 If they keep but to pay for their rent.
The poorest of all now do merrily call,
 When at a fit place they can stay,
For a song or a tale or a cup of good ale
 To drive the cold winter away.

Thus none will allow of solitude now
    But merrily greets the time,
To make it appear of all the whole year
    That this is accounted the prime:
December is seen apparel'd in green,
    And January fresh as May
Comes dancing along with a cup and a song
    To drive the cold winter away.

THE SECOND PART.

This time of the year is spent in good cheer,
    And neighbours together do meet
To sit by the fire, with friendly desire,
    Each other in love to greet;
Old grudges forgot are put in the pot,
    All sorrows aside they lay;
The old and the young doth carol this song
    To drive the cold winter away.

Sisley and Nanny, more jocund than any,
    As blithe as the month of June,
Do carol and sing like birds of the spring,
    No nightingale sweeter in tune;
To bring in content, when summer is spent,
    In pleasant delight and play,

With mirth and good cheer to end the whole year,
    And drive the cold winter away.

The shepherd, the swain do highly disdain
    To waste out their time in care,
And Clim of the Clough hath plenty enough
    If he but a penny can spare
To spend at the night, in joy and delight,
    Now after his labour all day ;
For better than lands is the help of his hands
    To drive the cold winter away.

To mask and to mum kind neighbours will come
    With wassails of nut-brown ale,
To drink and carouse to all in the house
    As merry as bucks in the dale ;
Where cake, bread, and cheese is brought for your fees
    To make you the longer stay ;
At the fire to warm 'twill do you no harm,
    To drive the cold winter away.

When Christmas's tide comes in like a bride
    With holly and ivy clad,
Twelve days in the year much mirth and good cheer
    In every household is had ;

The country guise is then to devise
  Some gambols of Christmas play,
Whereat the young men do best that they can
  To drive the cold winter away.

When white-bearded frost hath threatened his worst,
  And fallen from branch and briar,
Then time away calls from husbandry halls
  And from the good countryman's fire,
Together to go, to plough and to sow,
  To get us both food and array,
And thus with content the time we have spent
  To drive the cold winter away.

From Evans' Old Ballads, ed. 1810,
I. 146-150.

Old Christmas Returned,

OR, HOSPITALITY REVIVED ;

Being a Looking-glass for rich Misers, wherein they may see (if they
be not blind) how much they are to blame for their penurious
housekeeping, and likewise an encouragement to those noble-
minded gentry, who lay out a great part of their estates in hospitality, relieving such persons as have need thereof ;

"Who feasts the poor, a true reward shall find,
Or helps the old, the feeble, lame, and blind."

To the tune of " The Delights of the Bottle."

ALL you that to feasting and mirth are inclined,
C ome here is good news for to pleasure your
mind,
Old Christmas is come for to keep open house,
He scorns to be guilty of starving a mouse :
Then come, boys, and welcome for diet the chief,
Plum-pudding, goose, capon, minced pies, and roast-
beef.

A long time together he hath been forgot,
They scarce could afford to hang on the pot;
Such miserly sneaking in England hath been,
As by our forefathers ne'er us'd to be seen;
But now he's returned you shall have in brief,
Plum-pudding, goose, capon, minced pies, and roast-
  beef.

The times were ne'er good since Old Christmas was
  fled,
And all hospitality hath been so dead;
No mirth at our festivals late did appear,
They scarcely would part with a cup of March beer;
But now you shall have for the ease of your grief,
Plum-pudding, goose, capon, minced pies, and roast-
  beef.

The butler and baker, they now may be glad,
The times they are mended, though they have been
  bad;
The brewer, he likewise may be of good cheer,
He shall have good trading for ale and strong beer;
All trades shall be jolly, and have for relief,
Plum-pudding, goose, capon, minced pies, and roast-
  beef.

The holly and ivy about the walls wind,
And show that we ought to our neighbours be
  kind,
Inviting each other for pastime and sport,
And where we best fare, there we most do resort ;
We fail not of victuals, and that of the chief,
Plum-pudding, goose, capon, minced pies, and roast-
  beef.

The cooks shall be busied by day and by night,
In roasting and boiling, for taste and delight ;
Their senses in liquor that's nappy they'll steep,
Though they be afforded to have little sleep ;
They still are employed for to dress us in brief,
Plum-pudding, goose, capon, minced pies, and roast-
  beef.

Although the cold weather doth hunger provoke,
'Tis a comfort to see how the chimneys do smoke ;
Provision is making for beer, ale, and wine,
For all that are willing or ready to dine :
Then haste to the kitchen for diet the chief,
Plum-pudding, goose, capon, minced pies, and roast-
  beef.

All travellers, as they do pass on their way,
At gentlemen's halls are invited to stay,
Themselves to refresh, and their horses to rest,
Since that he must be Old Christmas's guest;
Nay, the poor shall not want, but have for relief,
Plum-pudding, goose, capon, minced pies, and roast-
beef.

Now Mock-beggar-hall it no more shall stand
empty,
But all shall be furnisht with freedom and plenty;
The hoarding old misers, who us'd to preserve
The gold in their coffers, and see the poor starve,
Must now spread their tables, and give them in
brief,
Plum-pudding, goose, capon, minced pies, and roast-
beef.

The court, and the city, and country are glad,
Old Christmas is come to cheer up the sad;
Broad pieces and guineas about now shall fly,
And hundreds be losers by cogging a die,
Whilst others are feasting with diet the chief,
Plum-pudding, goose, capon, minced pies, and roast-
beef.

Those that have no coin at the cards for to play,
May sit by the fire, and pass time away,
And drink of their moisture contented and free,
"My honest good fellow, come, here is to thee!"
And when they are hungry, fall to their relief,
Plum-pudding, goose, capon, minced pies, and roast-
    beef.

Young gallants and ladies shall foot it along,
Each room in the house to the music shall throng,
Whilst jolly carouses about they shall pass,
And each country swain trip about with his lass;
Meantime goes the caterer to fetch in the chief,
Plum-pudding, goose, capon, minced pies, and roast-
    beef.

The cooks and the scullion, who toil in their
    frocks,
Their hopes do depend upon their Christmas box;
There is very few that do live on the earth
But enjoy at this time either profit or mirth;
Yea those that are charged to find all relief,
Plum-pudding, goose, capon, minced pies, and roast-
    beef.

Then well may we welcome Old Christmas to town,
Who brings us good cheer, and good liquor so brown ;
To pass the cold winter away with delight,
We feast it all day, and we frolick all night ;
Both hunger and cold we keep out with relief,
Plum-pudding, goose, capon, minced pies, and roast-
beef.

Then let all curmudgeons who dote on their wealth,
And value their treasure much more than their health,
Go hang themselves up, if they will be so kind ;
Old Christmas with them but small welcome shall
find ;
They will not afford to themselves without grief,
Plum-pudding, goose, capon, minced pies, and roast-
beef.

From Round about our Coal Fire, 1740.

O you merry, merry Souls.

O YOU merry, merry Souls,
    Christmas is a-coming,
We shall have flowing bowls,
    Dancing, piping, drumming.

Delicate minced pies
    To feast every virgin,
Capon and goose likewise,
    Brawn and a dish of sturgeon.

Then, for your Christmas box,
    Sweet plum cakes and money,
Delicate holland smocks,
    Kisses sweet as honey.

Hey for the Christmas ball,
    Where we shall be jolly,
Jigging short and tall,
    Kate, Dick, Ralph, and Molly.

Then to the Hop we'll go
   Where we'll jig and caper ;
Maidens all-a-row ;
   Will shall pay the scraper.

Hodge shall dance with Prue,
   Keeping time with kisses ;
We'll have a jovial crew
   Of sweet smirking misses.

From Ritson's Ancient Songs, where it is stated to be from Wynkyn de Worde's Christmasse Carolles, 1521.

A Carol.

BRINGING IN THE BOAR'S HEAD.

CAPUT apri defero
    Reddens laudes domino.
The boar's head in hand bring I,
With garlands gay and rosemary;
I pray you all sing merrily
        Qui estis in convivio.

The boar's head, I understand,
Is the chief service in this land;
Look, wherever it be fand,
        Servite cum cantico.

Be glad, lords, both more and less,
  For this hath ordained our steward
To cheer you all this Christmas,
  The boar's head with mustard.

*A modern version of the previous Carol.
From Dibdin's Typog. Antiq.* ii.
252.

The Boar's Head Carol.

SUNG AT QUEEN'S COLLEGE, OXFORD.

THE boar's head in hand bear I,
    Bedecked with bays and rosemary;
And I pray you, my masters, be merry,
    Quot estis in convivo.
        *Caput apri defero
        Reddens laudes domino.*

The boar's head, as I understand,
Is the rarest dish in all this land,
Which thus bedeck'd with a gay garland
    Let us servire cantico.
        *Caput apri defero
        Reddens laudes domino.*

Our steward hath provided this
In honour of the King of bliss;
Which on this day to be served is
    In Reginensi Atrio.
        *Caput apri defero
        Reddens laudes domino.*

From the Christmas Prince, 1607 (printed in 1814).

Boar's Head Carol.

SUNG AT ST. JOHN'S COLLEGE, OXFORD, CHRISTMAS, 1607.

1. THE Boar is dead,
    Lo, here his head;
  What man could have done more
Than his head off to strike,
Meleager-like,
  And bring it as I do before.

2. He living spoiled
Where good men toiled,
  Which made kind Ceres sorry;
But now dead and drawn
Is very good brawn,
  And we have brought it for ye.

3. Then set down the swineyard,
The foe to the Vineyard,
  Let Bacchus crown his fall;
Let this boar's-head and mustard
Stand for pig, goose, and custard,
  And so ye are welcome all.

By Robert Herrick.

The Wassail.

GIVE way, give way, ye gates, and win
　　An easy blessing to your bin
And basket by our entering in.

May both with manchet stand replete ;
Your larders too so hung with meat
That, though a thousand thousand eat,

Yet, ere twelve moons shall whirl about
Their silvery spheres, there's none may doubt
But more's sent in than was serv'd out.

Next may your dairies prosper so
As that your pans no ebb may know ;
But if they do, the more to flow,

Like to a solemn sober stream,
Bank'd all with lilies and the cream
Of sweetest cowslips filling them.

Then may your plants be pressed with fruit,
Nor bee or hive you have be mute,
But sweetly sounding like a lute.

Next may your duck and teeming hen
Both to the cock's-tread say Amen,
And for their two eggs render ten.

Last, may your harrows, shares and ploughs,
Your stacks, your stocks, your sweetest mows,
All prosper by your virgin-vows.

Alas ! we bless, but see none here
That brings us either ale or beer :
In a dry house all things are near.

Let's leave a longer time to wait,
When rust and cobwebs bind the gate
And all live here with needy Fate.

Where chimneys do for ever weep
For want of warmth, and stomachs keep
With noise the servants' eyes from sleep.

It is in vain to sing or stay
Our free feet here ; but we'll away :
Yet to the Lares this we'll say,—

The time will come when you'll be sad
And reckon this for fortune bad,
T' have lost the good ye might have had.

From an undated black letter collection
of New Christmas Carols (pre-
served in the Bodleian Library).

Wassailing Song.

A JOLLY wassail bowl,
   A wassail of good ale;
Well fare the butler's soul .
   That setteth this to sale;
          Our jolly wassail.

Good dame, here at your door
   Our wassail we begin,
We are all maidens poor,
   We pray now let us in
          With our wassail.

Our wassail we do fill
   With apples and with spice,
Then grant us your good will
   To taste here once or twice
          Of our good wassail.

If any maidens be
   Here dwelling in this house,
They kindly will agree
   To take a full carouse
         Of our wassail.

But here they let us stand
   All freezing in the cold :
Good master, give command
   To enter and be bold,
         With our wassail.

Much joy into this hall
   With us is entered in,
Our master first of all
   We hope will now begin
         Of our wassail.

And after, his good wife
   Our spicèd bowl will try ;
The Lord prolong your life !
   Good fortune we espy
         For our wassail.

M

Some bounty from your hands
    Our wassail to maintain;
We'll buy no house nor lands
    With that which we do gain
                With our wassail.

This is our merry night
    Of choosing king and queen
Then be it your delight
    That something may be seen
                In our wassail.

It is a noble part
    To bear a liberal mind;
God bless our master's heart!
    For here we comfort find,
                With our wassail

And now we must begone
    To seek out more good cheer,
Where bounty will be shown
    As we have found it here,
                With our wassail

Much joy betide them all,
Our prayers shall be still,
We hope and ever shall
For this your great good will
To our wassail.

*This piece and the next were commu-
nicated to Notes and Queries (4th
series, ii. 551), by Cuthbert Bede.*

Wassailing Song.

WE wish you merry Christmas, also a glad New
     Year;
We come to bring you tidings to all mankind so dear;
We come to tell that Jesus was born in Bethl'em town,
And now he's gone to glory and pityingly looks
    down
          On us poor wassailers,
          As wassailing we go;
          With footsteps sore
          From door to door
       We trudge through sleet and snow.

A manger was his cradle, the straw it was his bed,
The oxen were around him within that lowly shed;
No servants waited on him with lords and ladies gay;
But now he's gone to glory and unto him we pray.
              Us poor wassailers, &c.

His mother loved and tended him and nursed him
    at her breast,
And good old Joseph watched them both the while
    they took their rest ;
And wicked Herod vainly sought to rob them of their
    child,
By slaughtering the Innocents in Bethlehem un-
    defiled.
                 But us poor wassailers, &c.

Now, all good Christian people, with great concern
    we sing
These tidings of your Jesus, the Saviour, Lord and
    King ;
In poverty he passed his days that riches we might
    share,
And of your wealth he bids you give and of your
    portion spare
                 To us poor wassailers, &c.

Your wife shall be a fruitful vine, a hus'sif good and
    able ;
Your children like the olive branches round about
    your table ;

Your barns shall burst with plenty and your crops shall
    be secure
If you will give your charity to us who are so poor.
                Us poor wassailers, &c.

And now no more we'll sing to you because the hour
    is late,
And we must trudge and sing our song at many another
    gate;
And so we'll wish you once again a merry Christmas
    time,
And pray God bless you while you give good silver
    for our rhyme.
                Us poor wassailers, &c.

here we come a Whistling.

HERE we come a whistling through the fields so
    green ;
Here we come a singing, so fair to be seen.
    God send you happy, God send you happy,
    Pray God send you a happy New Year !

The roads are very dirty, my boots are very thin,
I have a little pocket to put a penny in.
              God send you happy, &c.

Bring out your little table and spread it with a cloth,
Bring out some of your old ale, likewise your Christ-
    mas loaf,
              God send you happy, &c.

God bless the master of this house, likewise the mistress
    too ;
And all the little children that round the table strew.
              God send you happy, &c.

THE cock sat up in the yew tree,
　　The hen came chuckling by,
I wish you a merry Christmas,
　　And a good fat pig in the sty.

*From Chappell's Collection of ancient
English Melodies, p. 161. An-
other version is given in Hone's
Table Book, ii. 14.*

Wassail, wassail, all over the Town.

WASSAIL, wassail, all over the town,
    Our bread it is white, and our ale it is brown;
Our bowl it is made of the maplin tree,
So here, my good fellow, I'll drink it to thee.

The wassailing bowl, with a toast within,
Come, fill it up unto the brim;
Come fill it up that we may all see;
With the wassailing bowl I'll drink to thee.

Come, butler, come bring us a bowl of your best,
And we hope your soul in heaven shall rest;
But if you do bring us a bowl of your small,
Then down shall go butler, the bowl and all.

O butler, O butler, now don't you be worst,
But pull out your knife and cut us a toast;
And cut us a toast, one that we may all see;—
With the wassailing bowl I'll drink to thee.

Here's to Dobbin and to his right eye !
God send our mistress a good Christmas pie !
A good Christmas pie as e'er we did see ;—
With the wassailing bowl I'll drink to thee.

Here's to Broad May and to his broad horn,
God send our master a good crop of corn,
A good crop of corn as we all may see ;—
With the wassailing bowl I'll drink to thee.

Here's to Colly and to her long tail,
We hope our master and mistress heart will ne'er fail ;
But bring us a bowl of your good strong beer,
And then we shall taste of your happy new year.

Be there here any pretty maids? we hope there be
        some ;
Don't let the jolly wassailers stand on the cold stone,
But open the door and pull out the pin,
That we jolly wassailers may all sail in.

From Wright's Songs and Carols (Percy Society). An inferior version (from MS. Harl. 541) was printed by Ritson.

Bring us in good Ale.

BRING us in good ale, and bring us in good ale;
   For our blessed Lady's sake, bring us in good ale.

Bring us in no brown bread, for that is made of bran,
Nor bring us in no white bread, for therein is no game,
      But bring us in good ale.

Bring us in no beef, for there is many bones,
But bring us in good ale, for that goeth down at once;
      And bring us in good ale.

Bring us in no bacon, for that is passing fat,
But bring us in good ale, and give us enough of that;
      And bring us in good ale.

Bring us in no mutton, for that is often lean,
Nor bring us in no tripes, for they be seldom clean;
      But bring us in good ale.

Bring us in no eggs, for there are many shells,
But bring us in good ale, and give us nothing else ;
　　　And bring us in good ale.

Bring us in no butter, for therein are many hairs,
Nor bring us in no pig's flesh, for that will make us
　　　boars ;
　　　　　But bring us in good ale.

Bring us in no puddings, for therein is all God's good,
Nor bring us in no venison, for that is not for our
　　　blood ;
　　　　　But bring us in good ale.

Bring us in no capon's flesh, for that is ofte[n] dear,
Nor bring us in no duck's flesh, for they slobber in the
　　　mere ;
　　　　　But bring us in good ale.

*This and the three following pieces are
from New Christmas Carols, 1642.*

Come follow, follow me.

TO THE TUNE OF THE "SPANISH GIPSIES."

COME follow, follow me,
    Those that good fellows be,
Into the buttery
Our manhood for to try;
The Master keeps a bounteous house,
And gives leave freely to carouse.

Then wherefore should we fear,
Seeing here is store of cheer?
It shows but cowardice
At this time to be nice.
Then boldly draw your blades and fight,
For we shall have a merry night.

When we have done this fray,
Then we will go to play

At cards or else at dice,
And be rich in a trice ;
Then let the knaves go round apace,
I hope each time to have an ace.

Come, maids, let's want no beer
After our Christmas cheer,
And I will duly crave
Good husbands you may have,
And that you may good houses keep,
Where we may drink carouses deep.

And when that's spent the day
We'll Christmas gambols play,
At hot cockles beside
And then go to all-hide,
With many other pretty toys,
Men, women, youths, maids, girls and boys.

Come, let's dance round the hall,
And let's for liquor call ;
Put apples in the fire,
Sweet maids, I you desire ;
And let a bowl be spiced well
Of happy stuff that doth excel.

Twelve days we now have spent
In mirth and merriment,
And daintily did fare,
For which we took no care ;
But now I sadly call to mind
What days of sorrow are behind.

We must leave off to play,
To morrow's working-day ;
According to each calling
Each man must now be falling,
And ply his business all the year,
Next Christmas for to make good cheer,

Now of my master kind
Good welcome I did find,
And of my loving mistress
This merry time of Christmas ;
For which to them great thanks I give,
God grant they long together live.

All you that are good Fellows.

ALL you that are good fellows
　　Come hearken to my song;
I know you do not hate good cheer
　　Nor liquor that is strong.
I hope there is none here
　　But soon will take my part,
Seeing my master and my dame
　　Says welcome with their heart.

This is a time of joyfulness
　　And merry time of year,
Whereas the rich with plenty stored
　　Doth make the poor good cheer;
Plum-porridge, roast-beef, and minced pies
　　Stand smoking on the board,
With other brave varieties
　　Our master doth afford.

Our mistress and her cleanly maids
   Have neatly played the cooks ;
Methinks these dishes eagerly
   At my sharp stomach looks,
As though they were afraid
   To see me draw my blade,
But I revenged on them will be
   Until my stomach's stayed.

Come fill us of the strongest,
   Small drink is out of date,
Methinks I shall fare like a prince
   And sit in gallant state :
This is no miser's feast,
   Although that things be dear ;
God grant the founder of this feast
   Each Christmas keep good cheer.

This day for Christ we celebrate
   Who was born at this time ;
For which all Christians should rejoice
   And I do sing in rhyme.
When you have given God thanks,
   Unto your dainties fall :
Heaven bless my master and my dame,
   Lord bless me and you all.

N

Come, mad Boys.

To the tune of " Bonny Sweet Robin."

COME, mad boys, be glad, boys, for Christmas is
        here,
And we shall be feasted with jolly good cheer;
Then let us be merry, 'tis Saint Stephen's day,
Let's eat and drink freely, here's nothing to pay.

My master bids welcome, and so doth my dame,
And 'tis yonder smoking dish doth me inflame;
Anon I'll be with you, though you me outface,
For now I do tell you I have time and place.

I'll troll the bowl to you, then let it go round,
My heels are so light they can stand on no ground;
My tongue it doth chatter, and goes pitter patter,
Here's good beer and strong beer, for I will not
        flatter.

And now for remembrance of blessed Saint Stephen,
Let's joy at morning, at noon, and at even ;[1]
Then leave off your mincing, and fall to mince-pies,
I pray take my counsel, be ruled by the wise.

---

[1] Old ed. "evening."

Come bravely on, my Masters.

To the tune of " The King's going to Bulleine."

COME bravely on, my masters,
   For here we shall be tasters
Of curious dishes that are brave and fine,
Where they that do such cheer afford,
I'll lay my knife upon the board,
   My master and my dame they do not pine.

Who is't will not be merry
And sing down, down, aderry?
   For now it is a time of joy and mirth;
'Tis said 'tis merry in the hall
When as beards they do wag all;
   God's plenty's here, it doth not show a dearth.

Let him take all lives longest,
Come fill us of the strongest,
   And I will drink a health to honest John;
Come pray thee, butler, fill the bowl,
And let it round the table troll,
   When that is up I'll tell you more anon.

From New Christmas Carols (no date).

My Master and Dame, I well perceive.

To the tune of "Green Sleeves."

MY master and dame, I well perceive,
 Are purposed to be merry to-night,
And willingly hath given me leave
 To combat with a Christmas Knight.
Sir Pig, I see, comes prancing in
 And bids me draw if that I dare ;
I care not for his valour a pin,
 For Jack of him will have a share.

My lady goose among the rest
 Upon the table takes her place,
And piping-hot bids do my best,
 And bravely looks me in the face ;
For pigs and geese are gallant cheer,
 God bless my master and dame therefore !
I trust before the next New Year
 To eat my part of half a score.

I likewise see good minced-pie
   Here standing swaggering on the table;
The lofty walls so large and high
   I'll level down if I be able;
For they be furnished with good plums,
   And spiced well with pepper and salt,
Every prune as big as both my thumbs
   To drive down bravely the juice of malt.

Fill me some of your Christmas beer,
   Your pepper sets my mouth on heat,
And Jack's a-dry with your good cheer,
   Give me some good ale to my meat.
And then again my stomach I'll show,
   For good roast-beef here stoutly stands;
I'll make it stoop before I go,
   Or I'll be no man of my hands.

And for the plenty of this house
   God keep it thus well-stored alway;
Come, butler, fill me a good carouse,
   And so we'll end our Christmas day.

This piece and the next are from New Christmas Carols, 1661.

With merry Glee and Solace.

FOR ST. STEPHEN'S DAY.

To the tune of "Henry's going to Bullen.'

WITH merry glee and solace
    This second day of Christmas
Now comes in bravely to my master's house,
Where plenty of good cheer I see,
With that which most contenteth me,
As brawn and bacon, powdered beef and souse.

For the love of Stephen,
That blessed saint of heaven,
Which stonèd was [for] Jesus Christ his sake,
Let us all both more and less
Cast away all heaviness,
And in a sober manner merry make.

He was a man beloved,
And his faith approved
By suffering death on this holy day,
Where he with gentle patience
And a constant sufferance,
Hath taught us all to heaven the ready way.[1]

So let our mirth be civil,
That not one thought of evil
May take possession of our hearts at all,
So shall we love and favour get
Of them that kindly thus do set
Their bounties here so freely in this hall.

Of delicates so dainty,
I see now here is plenty
Upon this table ready here prepared;
Then let us now give thanks to those
That all things friendly thus bestows,
Esteeming not this world that is so hard.

For of the same my master
Hath made me here a taster;

---

[1] The old ed. gives " Hath taught to us all heaven," &c.

The Lord above requite him for the same !
And so to all within this house
I will drink a full carouse,
With leave of my good master and my dame.

And the Lord be praised
My stomach is well eased,
My bones at quiet may go take their rest ;
Good fortune surely followed me
To bring me thus so luckily
To eat and drink so freely of the best.

In honour of Saint John we thus.

(FOR ST. JOHN'S DAY.)

To the tune of " Sellenger's Round."

IN honour of Saint John we thus
　　Do keep good Christmas cheer ;
And he that comes to dine with us,
　　I think he need not spare.
The butcher he hath killed good beef,
　　The caterer brings it in ;
But Christmas pies are still the chief,
　　If that I durst begin.

Our bacon-hogs are full and fat
　　To make us brawn and souse ;
Full well may I rejoice thereat
　　To see them in the house.

But yet the minced pie it is
　　That sets my teeth on water ;
Good mistress, let me have a bit,
　　For I do long thereafter.

And I will fetch your water in
　　To brew and bake withal,
Your love and favour still to win
　　When as you please to call.
Then grant me, dame, your love and leave
　　To taste your pie-meat here ;
It is the best in my conceit
　　Of all your Christmas-cheer.

The cloves and mace and gallant plums [1]
　　That here on heaps do lie,
[And prunes] as big as both my thumbs,
　　Enticeth much mine eye.
Oh, let me eat my belly-full
　　Of your good Christmas-pie ;
Except thereat I have a pull,
　　I think I sure shall die.

Good master, stand my loving friend,
　　For Christmas-time is short,

---

[1] Old ed. "prunes."—Cf. p. 198, ll. 5-7.

And when it comes unto an end
   I may no longer sport ;
Then while it doth continue here
   Let me such labour find,
To eat my fill of that good cheer
   That best doth please my mind.

Then I shall thank my dame therefore,
   That gives her kind consent,
That Jack your boy with others more
   May have this Christmas spent
In pleasant mirth and merry glee,
   As young men most delight ;
For that's the only sport for me,
   And so God give you all good-night.

From New Christmas Carols (no date).

The New Year is begun.

THE SHEPHERD'S CAROL TO BE SUNG ON NEW YEAR'S
DAY.

Tune, " Humming of the Drone."

THE New Year is begun,
  Good morrow, my masters all !
The cheerful rising sun
  Now shining in this hall,
    Brings mirth and joy
    To man and boy.
With all that here doth dwell ;
    Whom Jesus bless
    With love's increase,
So all things shall prosper well.

A New Year's gift I bring
  Unto my master here,
Which is a welcome thing
  Of mirth and merry cheer.

A New Year's lamb
Come from thy dam
An hour before daybreak,
Your noted ewe
Doth this bestow,
Good master, for your sake.

And to my dame so kind
This New Year's gift I bring;
I'll bear an honest mind
Unto her whilst I live.
Your white-wooled sheep
I'll safely keep
From harm of bush or brere,[1]
That garments gay
For your array
May clothe you the next New Year.

And to your children all,
These New Year's gifts I bring;
And though the price be small,
They're fit for queen or king:
Fair pippins red
Kept in my bed

---

[1] Old ed. " Bryar."

A-mellowing since last year,
    Whose beauty bright
    So clear of sight
Their hearts will glad and cheer.

And to your maids and men
    I bring both points and pins ;
Come bid me welcome then,
    The good New Year begins :
        And for my love
        Let me approve
The friendship of your Maid,
        Whose nappy ale
        So good and stale
Will make my wits afraid.

I dare not with it deal
    But in a sober diet :
If I poor shepherd steal
    A draught to be unquiet,
        And lose my way
        This New Year's day
As I go to my fold,
        You'll surely think
        My love of drink
This following year will hold.

Here stands my bottle and hook,
 Good kitchen-maid, draw near,
Thou art an honest cook,
 And canst brew ale and beer ;
  Thy office show,
  Before I go,
My bottle and bag come fill,
  And for thy sake
  I'll merry make
Upon the next green hill.

From A Cabinet of Choice Jewels, or
the Christian's Joy and Gladness,
1688.

The Young Men and Maids on New Year's Day.

Tune of "Caper and jerk it."

THE young men and maids on New Year's day,
 Their loves they will present
With many a gift both fine and gay,
 Which gives them true content :
And though the gift be great or small,
 Yet this is the custom still,
Expressing their loves in ribbons and gloves,
 It being their kind good-will.

Young bachelors will not spare their coin,
 But thus their love is shown ;
Young Richard will buy a bodkin fine
 And give it honest Joan.
There's Nancy and Sue with honest Prue,
 Young damsels both fair and gay,
Will give to the men choice presents agen
 For the honour of New Year's day.

O

Fine ruffs, cravats of curious lace,
　Maids give them fine and neat;
For this the young men will them embrace
　With tender kisses sweet:
And give them many pleasant toys
　To deck them fine and gay,
As bodkins and rings with other fine things
　For the honour of New Year's day.

It being the first day of the year,
　To make the old amends,
All those that have it will dress good cheer
　Inviting all their friends.
To drink great James's royal health,
　As very well subjects may,
With many healths more, which we have store,
　For the honour of New Year's day.

From New Christmas Carols, 1642.

The Old Year now away is fled.

To the tune of " Green Sleeves."

THE old year now away is fled,
   The new year it is entered,
Then let us now our sins down tread
   And joyfully all appear.
Let's merry be this holiday,
And let us now both sport and play,
Hang sorrow, let's cast care away :
   God send you a happy New Year !

For Christ's circumcision this day we keep,
Who for our sins did often weep ;
His hands and feet were wounded deep,
   And his blessed side, with a spear.
His head they crowned then with thorn,
And at him they did laugh and scorn,
Who for to save our souls was born ;
   God send us a happy New Year !

And now with New-Year's gifts each friend
Unto each other they do send;
God grant we may all our lives amend,
   And that the truth may appear.
Now like the snake cast-off your skin
Of evil thoughts and wicked sin,
And to amend this New Year begin:
   God send us a merry New Year!

And now let all the company
In friendly manner all agree,
For we are here welcome, all may see,
   Unto this jolly good cheer.
I thank my master and my dame,
The which are founders of the same;
To eat, to drink now is no shame:
   God send us a merry New Year!

Come lads and lasses every one,
Jack, Tom, Dick, Bessy, Mary and Joan,
Let's cut the meat up unto the bone,
   For welcome you need not fear;
And here for good liquor we shall not lack,
It will whet my brains and strengthen my back;
This jolly good cheer it must go to wrack:
   God send us a merry New Year!

Come, give's more liquor when I do call,
I'll drink to each one in this hall ;
I hope that so loud I must not bawl,
 But unto me lend an ear ;
Good fortune to my master send,
And to my dame which is our friend,
Lord bless us all, and so I end :
 God send us a happy New Year !

From Poor Robin's Almanac, 1664.

Provide for Christmas.

PROVIDE for Christmas ere that it do come,
　　To feast thy neighbour good cheer to have
　　some;
Good bread and drink, a fire in the hall,
Brawn, pudding, souse and good mustard withal;
Beef, mutton, pork, and shred pies of the best,
Pig, veal, goose, capon, and turkey well drest;
Apples and nuts to throw about the hall,
That boys and girls may scramble for them all.
Sing jolly carols, make the fiddlers play,
Let scrupulous fanatics keep away;
For oftentimes seen no arranter knave
Than some who do counterfeit most to be grave.

From Poor Robin's Almanac, 1695.

Now thrice welcome, Christmas.

NOW thrice welcome, Christmas,
　　Which brings us good cheer,
Minced pies and plum porridge,
　　Good ale and strong beer;
With pig, goose and capon,
　　The best that may be,
So well doth the weather
　　And our stomachs agree.

Observe how the chimneys
　　Do smoke all about,
The cooks are providing
　　For dinner, no doubt;
But those on whose tables
　　No victuals appear,
O may they keep Lent
　　All the rest of the year.

With holly and ivy
　So green and so gay,
We deck up our houses
　As fresh as the day ;
With bay and rosemary
　And laurel complete ;
And every one now
　Is a king in conceit.

From Poor Robin's Almanac, 1700.

Now that the time is come wherein.

NOW that the time is come wherein
　　Our Saviour Christ was born,
The larders full of beef and pork,
　　The garners fill'd with corn;
As God hath plenty to thee sent,
　　Take comfort of thy labours,
And let it never thee repent
　　To feast thy needy neighbours.

Let fires in every chimney be
　　That people they may warm them;
Tables with dishes covered,—
　　Good victuals will not harm them.
With mutton, veal, beef, pig and pork,
　　Well furnish every board;
Plum-pudding, furmity and what
　　Thy stock will them afford.

No niggard of thy liquor be,
   Let it go round thy table;
People may freely drink, but not
   So long as they are able.
Good customs they may be abused,
   Which makes rich men to slack us;
This feast is to relieve the poor
   And not to drunken Bacchus.

Thus if thou doest
   'Twill credit raise thee;
God will thee bless
   And neighbours praise thee.

From Poor Robin's Almanac, 1701.

Now enter Christmas like a man.

NOW enter Christmas like a man,
    Armed with spit and dripping-pan,
Attended with pasty, plum-pie,
Puddings, plum-porridge, furmity ;
With beef, pork, mutton of each sort
More than my pen can make report ;
Pig, swan, goose, rabbits, partridge, teal,
With legs and loins and breasts of veal :
But above all the minced pies
Must mention'd be in any wise,
Or else my Muse were much to blame,
Since they from Christmas take their name.
With these, or any one of these,
A man may dine well if he please ;
Yet this must well be understood,—
Though one of these be singly good,
Yet more the merrier is the best
As well of dishes as of guest.

    But the times are grown so bad
Scarce one dish for the poor is had ;

Good housekeeping is laid aside,
And all is spent to maintain pride;
Good works are counted popish, and
Small charity is in the land.
A man may sooner (truth I tell ye)
Break his own neck than fill his belly.
Good God, amend what is amiss
And send a remedy to this,
That Christmas day again may rise
And we enjoy our Christmas pies.

From Poor Robin's Almanac, 1715.

Now Christmas comes 'tis fit that we.

NOW Christmas comes, 'tis fit that we
　　Should feast and sing and merry be,
Keep open house, let fiddlers play;
A fig for cold, sing care away!
And may they who thereat repine,
On brown bread and on small beer dine.
Make fires with logs, let the cooks sweat
With boiling and with roasting meat;
Let ovens be heat for fresh supplies
Of puddings, pasties, and minced pies,
And whilst that Christmas doth abide
Let butt'ry-door stand open wide.
Hang up those churls that will not feast
Or with good fellows be a guest,
And hang up those would take away
The observation of that day;
O may they never minced pies eat,
Plum-pudding, roast-beef, nor such meat.

But blest be they, awake and sleep,
Who at that time [a] good house keep
May never want come nigh their door,
Who at that time relieve the poor;
Be plenty always in their house
Of beef, veal, lamb, pork, mutton, souse.

From the Bishoprick Garland, 1834 (a
collection of songs, ballads, etc.,
belonging to the county of Durham).

Maids, get up and Bake your Pies.

MAIDS, get up and bake your pies,
    Bake your pies, bake your pies ;
Maids, get up and bake your pies,
    'Tis Christmas day in the morning.

See the ships all sailing by,
    Sailing by, sailing by ;
See the ships all sailing by
    On Christmas day in the morning.

DAME, what made your ducks to die,
    Ducks to die, ducks to die ;
Dame, what made your ducks to die
    On Christmas day in the morning?

You let your lazy maidens lie,
  Maidens lie, maidens lie ;
You let your lazy maidens lie
  On Christmas day in the morning.

From Thomas Weelkes' Madrigals, 1597.

To shorten Winter's sadness.

TO shorten winter's sadness
   See where the nymphs with gladness
Disguised all are coming,
Right wantonly a mumming.
                 Fa la.

Whilst youthful sports are lasting,
To feasting turn our fasting;
With revels and with wassails
Make grief and care our vassals.
                 Fa la.

For youth it well beseemeth
That pleasure he esteemeth;
And sullen age is hated
That mirth would have abated.
                 Fa la.

By Robert Herrick.

A New Year's Gift sent to Sir Simeon Steward.

NO news of navies burnt at seas;
No noise of late-spawned tittyries;
No closet-plot or open vent
That frights men with a parliament;
No new device or late-found trick
To read by th' stars the kingdom's sick;
No gin to catch the state or ring
The free-born nostrils of the king,
We send to you: but here a jolly
Verse, crown'd with ivy and with holly,
That tells of winter's tales and mirth
That milk-maids make about the hearth;
Of Christmas-sports; the wassail bowl;
That tost up, after fox-i'-th'-hole;
Of blind-man's-buff, and of the care
That young men have to shoe the mare;
Of Twelfth-tide cakes, of pease and beans,
Wherewith ye make those merry scenes,

Whenas ye chuse your king and queen
And cry out *Hey for our town-green!*
Of ash-heaps, in the which ye use
Husbands and wives by streaks to chuse;
Of cracking laurel, which foresounds
A plenteous harvest to your grounds:
Of these and such like things, for shift,
We send instead of New-Year's gift.
Read then, and when your faces shine
With buxom meat and cap'ring wine,
Remember us in cups full-crown'd
And let our city-health go round,
Quite though the young maids and the men
To the ninth number, if not ten;
Until the fired chestnuts leap
For joy to see the fruits ye reap
From the plump chalice and the cup,
That tempts till it be tossèd up;
Then, as ye sit about your embers,
Call not to mind those fled Decembers,
But think on these that are t'appear
As daughters to the instant year.
Sit crowned with rose-buds, and carouse
Till Liber Pater twirls the house
About your ears, and lay upon
The year, your cares, that's fled and gone.

And let the russet swains the plough
And harrow hang up resting now,
And to the bagpipe all address
Till sleep takes place of weariness.
And thus throughout with Christmas plays
Frolic the full twelve holidays.

By Robert Herrick.

Twelfth Night;

OR, KING AND QUEEN.

NOW, now the mirth comes,
　　With the cake full of plums,
Where bean's the king of the sport here;
　　Beside we must know,
　　The pea also
Must revel as queen in the court here.

　　Begin then to chuse,
　　This night as ye use,
Who shall for the present delight here;
　　Be a king by the lot,
　　And who shall not
Be Twelfth-day queen for the night here.

　　Which known, let us make
　　Joy-sops with the cake;
And let not a man then be seen here
　　Who unurg'd will not drink,
　　To the base from the brink,
A health to the king and the queen here.

Next crown the bowl full
With gentle lambs-wool;
Add sugar, nutmeg, and ginger,
With store of ale too;
And thus ye must do
To make the wassail a swinger.

Give then to the king
And queen wassailing,
And though with ale ye be whet here,
Yet part ye from hence,
As free from offence,
As when ye innocent met here.

From Sir Walter Scott's Marmion.
(*Introduction to Canto VI.*)

Christmas in the Olden Time.

THE damsel donned her kirtle sheen ;
　The hall was dressed with holly green ;
Forth to the wood did merry-men go
To gather in the misletoe.
Then opened wide the baron's hall
To vassal, tenant, serf and all ;
Power laid his rod of rule aside,
And ceremony doffed his pride.
The heir, with roses in his shoes,
That night might village-partner chuse ;
The lord underogating share
The vulgar game of post-and-pair.
All hailed with uncontrolled delight
And general voice, the happy night,
That to the cottage as the crown
Brought tidings of salvation down.
The fire with well-dried logs supplied
Went roaring up the chimney wide ;

The huge hall-table's oaken face,
Scrubbed till it shone, the day to grace,
Bore then upon its massive board
No mark to part the squire and lord.
Then was brought in the lusty brawn
By old blue-coated serving-man ;
Then the grim boar's head frowned on high,
Crested with bay and rosemary.
Well can the green-garbed ranger tell
How, when, and where the monster fell ;
What dogs before his death he tore,
And all the baiting of the boar.
The wassail round, in good brown bowls,
Garnished with ribbons blithely trowls.
There the huge sir-loin reeked ; hard by
Plum-porridge stood and Christmas pie ;
Nor failed old Scotland to produce
At such high tide her savoury goose.
Then came the merry masquers in
And carols roared with blithesome din ;
If unmelodious was the song
It was a hearty note and strong.
Who lists may in their mumming see
Traces of ancient mystery ;
White shirts supplied the masquerade,
And smutted cheeks the visors made :

But, oh ! what masquers richly dight
Can boast of bosoms half so light !
England was merry England when
Old Christmas brought his sports again.
'Twas Christmas broached the mightiest ale,
'Twas Christmas told the merriest tale ;
A Christmas gambol oft would cheer
The poor man's heart through half the year.

*Dedication of Wordsworth's River Dud-
don Sonnets. Addressed to his
brother, Dr. Christopher Wordsworth.*

Christmas Minstrelsy.

THE minstrels played their Christmas tune
    To-night beneath my cottage eaves ;
While smitten by a lofty moon,
The encircling laurels thick with leaves,
Gave back a rich and dazzling sheen,
That overpowered their natural green.

Through hill and valley every breeze
Had sunk to rest with folded wings :
Keen was the air, but could not freeze
Nor check the music of the strings ;
So stout and hardy were the band
That scraped the chords with strenuous hand.

And who but listened ?—till was paid
Respect to every inmate's claim,
The greeting given, the music played
In honour of each household name,
Duly pronounced with lusty call,
And a merry Christmas wished to all.

O Brother! I revere the choice
That took thee from thy native hills;
And it is given thee to rejoice:
Though public care full often tills
(Heaven only witness of the toil)
A barren and ungrateful soil.

Yet would that thou, with me and mine,
Hadst heard this never-failing rite;
And seen on other faces shine
A true revival of the light;
Which nature, and these rustic powers,
In simple childhood, spread through ours!

For pleasure hath not ceased to wait
On these expected annual rounds,
Whether the rich man's sumptuous gate
Call forth the unelaborate sounds,
Or they are offered at the door
That guards the lowliest of the poor.

How touching, when at midnight, sweep
Snow-muffled winds, and all is dark,
To hear—and sink again to sleep!
Or at an earlier call, to mark,
By blazing fire, the still suspense
Of self-complacent innocence;

The mutual nod—the grave disguise
Of hearts with gladness brimming o'er,
And some unhidden tears that rise
For names once heard, and heard no more;
Tears brightened by the serenade
For infant in the cradle laid!

Ah! not for emerald fields alone,
With ambient streams more pure and bright
Than fabled Cytherea's zone
Glittering before the Thunderer's sight,
Is to my heart of hearts endeared,
The ground where we were born and reared!

Hail ancient manners! sure defence,
Where they survive, of wholesome laws:
Remnants of love whose modest sense
Thus into narrow room withdraws;
Hail usages of pristine mould,
And ye that guard them, mountains old!

Bear with me, Brother! quench the thought
That slights this passion or condemns;
If thee fond fancy ever brought
From the proud margin of the Thames,
And Lambeth's venerable towers,
To humbler streams and greener bowers.

Yes they can make, who fail to find,
Short leisure even in busiest days ;
Moments to cast a look behind,
And profit by those kindly rays
That through the clouds do sometimes steal,
And all the far-off past reveal.

Hence, while the imperial city's din
Beats frequent on thy satiate ear,
A pleased attention I may win
To agitations less severe,
That neither overwhelm nor cloy,
But fill the hollow vale with joy !

FAREWELL TO CHRISTMAS.

From New Christmas Carols, 1642.

Mark well my heavy doleful Tale.

To the tune of "The Lady's Fall."

MARK well my heavy doleful tale,
　　For Twelfth-day now is come,
And now I must no longer sing,
　　And say no words but mum;
For I perforce must take my leave
　　Of all my dainty cheer,
Plum-porridge, roast beef, and minced pies,
　　My strong ale and my beer.

Kind-hearted Christmas, now adieu,
　　For I with thee must part,
And for to take my leave of thee
　　Doth grieve me at the heart;

Thou wert an ancient housekeeper,
    And mirth with meat didst keep,
But thou art going out of town,
    Which makes me for to weep.

God knoweth whether I again
    Thy merry face shall see,
Which to good-fellows and the poor
    That was so frank and free.
Thou lovedst pastime with thy heart,
    And eke good company;
Pray hold me up for fear I swoon,
    For I am like to die.

Come, butler, fill a brimmer up
    To cheer my fainting heart,
That to old Christmas I may drink
    Before he doth depart;
And let each one that's in this room
    With me likewise condole,
And for to cheer their spirits sad
    Let each one drink a bowl.

And when the same it hath gone round
    Then fall unto your cheer,
For you do know that Christmas time
    It comes but once a year.

But this good draught which I have drunk
   Hath comforted my heart,
For I was very fearful that
   My stomach would depart.

Thanks to my master and my dame
   That doth such cheer afford;
God bless them, that each Christmas they
   May furnish thus their board.
My stomach having come to me,
   I mean to have a bout,
Intending to eat most heartily;
   Good friends, I do not flout.

Q

This piece and the next are from New Christmas Carols, 1661.

Now Farewell, Good Christmas.

To the tune of "Bonny Sweet Robin."

NOW farewell, good Christmas,
  Adieu and adieu,
I needs now must leave thee,
  And look for a new;
For till thou returnest,
  I linger in pain,
And I care not how quickly
  Thou comest again.

But ere thou departest
  I purpose to see
What merry good pastime
  This day will show me;
For a king of the wassail
  This night we must choose,
Or else the old customs
  We carelessly lose.

The wassail well spiced
　About shall go round,
Though it cost my good master
　Best part of a pound :
The maid in the buttery
　Stands ready to fill
Her nappy good liquor
　With heart and good will.

And to welcome us kindly
　Our master stands by,
And tells me in friendship
　One tooth is a-dry.
Then let us accept it
　As lovingly, friends ;
And so for this twelfth-day
　My carol here ends.

Christmas hath made an End.

To the tune of "Well a day."

CHRISTMAS hath made an end,
   Welladay, welladay,
Which was my dearest friend,
   More is the pity;
For with a heavy heart
   Must I from thee depart,
To follow plough and cart
   All the year after.

Lent is fast coming on,
   Welladay, welladay,
That loves not any one,
   More is the pity;
For I doubt both my cheeks
   Will look thin, eating leeks;
Wise is he then that seeks
   For a friend in a corner.

All our good cheer is gone,
　Welladay, welladay,
And turned to a bone,
　More is the pity.
In my good master's house
　I shall eat no more souse,
Then give me one carouse,
　Gentle, kind butler.

It grieves me to the heart,
　Welladay, welladay,
From my friend to depart,
　More is the pity.
Christmas, I mean, 'tis thee
　That thus forsaketh me,
Yet till one hour I see
　Will I be merry.

NOTES.

NOTES.

Page 1 : "*In every place*," &c.—These lines are spoken by Salomee. For disbelieving that the Child had been born of a virgin, her hand was withered up; but on her repentance God sent an angel who bade her worship the Child and touch his clothes. She obeyed, and her hand was restored; whereupon she raised this hymn of praise.

Page 4 : "*I sing of a maiden*."—This perfect little poem will be new to most readers. It has been passed over by the collectors.

Page 17 : "*You shall well see that kingès three*," &c.—The names of the three kings were Melchior, Gaspar, and Balthazar. The first was old, with grey hair and a long beard : his offering was gold. Gaspar, who was young and beardless, brought frankincense; and Balthazar, who was of a swarthy complexion, offered myrrh. Gold was symbolical of kingship, frankincense of divinity, and myrrh of humanity. The bodies of the three kings were taken, about three hundred years after their death, by the Empress Helena to Constantinople; thence by Eustatius to Milan; afterwards by Renaldus the bishop to Cologne, or Collein. Hence they were commonly called the Three Kings of Collein. There is an old carol about the Three Kings. Wright, in his collection of "Songs and Carols" published by the Percy Society, has printed one version of it; but the text of the following copy (from *Notes and Queries*, 6th Series, vi. 505-7) is fuller and more accurate :—

" Now is Christmas y-come,
Father and Son together in one,
Holy Ghost us be on
        In fere-a ; [1]
God send us a happy New Year-a !

I would you sing for, and I might,
Of a Child is fair in sight ;
His mother him bare this Yulès night
        So still-a,
And as it was his will-a.

There came three kings from Galilee
Into Bethlem that fair citie,
To seek Him that e'er should be
        By right-a
Lord and king and knight-a.

As they came forth with their off'ring,
They met with Herod that moody king
        This tide-a,
And this to them he said-a.

' Of whence be ye, you kingès three ? '
' Of the East, as you may see,
To worship Him that e'er should be
        By right-a
Lord and king and knight-a.'

' When you at this Child have be,
Come home again by me ;
Tell me the sight that you have see ;
        I pray you,
Go you none other way-a.'

---

[1] In fere = in company.

They took their leave both old and young
Of Herod that moody king;
They went forth with their offering
　　　　By light-a,
　　The star that shone so bright-a.

Till they came into the place
There Jesu and his mother was;
Offered they up with great solace
　　　　In fere-a
　　Gold and 'cense and myrrh-a.

The Father of heaven an angel sent
To these three kings that made present
　　　　This tide-a,
　　And this to them he said-a :—

' My Lord have warned you every one
By Herod king you go not home,
For and you do he will you slone [1]
　　　　And 'stroy-a,
　　And hurt you wonderly-a.'

Forth they went these kingès three
Till they came home to their countrie;
Glad and blithe they were all three
Of the sight that they had see;
　　　　　By dene-a [2]
　　The company was clean-a.

Kneel we now here a-down;
Pray we in good devotion
To the King of great renown,
　　　　Of grace-a
　　In heaven to have a place-a."

---

[1] Slay.　　　　[2] By dene = immediately.

(The last line of the penultimate stanza seems somewhat unintelligible.)

Page 19 : " *Tyrle, tyrle, so merrily,*" &c.—Compare a song in the Coventry Mysteries :—

> "As I rode out this endnes night
> Of three jolly shepherds I saw a sight,
> And all about their fold a star shone bright :
> They sang terli terlow,
> So merrily the shepherds their pipes can blow."

Page 21 : " *This endnes night.*"—The MS. from which this piece is taken contains a large collection of church-services, hymns, carols, and songs,—with music. It formerly belonged to Joseph Ritson, who presented it to the British Museum. The collection deserves to be printed in full.

Page 25 : " *As I sat under a sycamore tree.*"—This is a variation of the very common carol, " As I sat on a sunny bank."

Page 26 : William Byrd, a celebrated musician, was born about 1545, and died in 1623. The reader will find an account of his works in Oliphant's Musa Madrigalesca. Probably Byrd wrote only the music for his collections.

Page 29 : " *Joseph was an old man.*"—I do not feel at all sure that I have done right in dividing this carol into three parts. Perhaps it would have been better to print Part II. as a separate piece, and join Part III. to Part I. As regards the text of this carol no two copies are found to agree, and one is obliged to adopt an eclectic method. The alterations made by modern editors in deference to the mock-modesty of the day are singularly flat. Mr. Bramley, in " Christmas Carols New and Old," gives the following ridiculous rendering of the fourth and fifth stanzas :—

> " Mary said to Joseph
> With her sweet lips so mild,
> Pluck those cherries, Joseph,
> For to give to my Child.
>
> O then replied Joseph,
> With words so unkind,
> I will pluck no cherries
> For to give to thy Child."

Could anything be more pointless? Hone, in his Ancient Mysteries (p. 90), gives after the first stanza—

> " When Joseph was married,
> And his cousin Mary got,
> Mary proved big with child,
> By whom Joseph knew not."

After the penultimate stanza some copies add—

> " And upon a Wednesday
> My vow I will make,
> And upon Good Friday
> My death I will take."

Page 33 : " *St. Stephen was a clerk.*"—We learn from Dr. Prior's "Ancient Danish Ballads" (I. 395) that the oldest account of the singular legend which is the subject of this carol " is in Vinc. Bellovacensis, from an author who lived about 1200. Two friends sat down to dinner in Bologna, and one bade the other to carve the cock, which he did, so that, as he said, not St. Peter or our Lord himself could put it together again. The cock sprang up, clapped his wings and crowed, scattering the sauce over the two friends, and rendering them lepers till the day of their death. The same miracle is related as having occurred to prove the innocence of persons falsely accused, and is found in the legends of Spain Brittany, Italy, and Slavonian countries.   How it came to be appropriated to St. Stephen does not appear."

Page 36 : "*Remember, O thou man.*"—A different version of this carol is given in Mr. Thomas Hardy's " Under the Greenwood Tree."

Page 40 : "*God rest you merry, gentlemen.*"—The comma, by a curious oversight, has been misplaced.   It should stand before, not after, the word " merry."

Page 48 : "*Nay, Nay, sweet Jesus said,*" &c.—I have ventured to end the carol with this stanza.   In all the copies that I have seen an additional stanza follows—

> "O then spoke the angel Gabriel,
>   Upon one good Saint Stephen,
> Although you're but a maiden's child,
>   You are the King of heaven."

The conclusion is spoiled by the introduction of these mysterious lines, which have no connection with the context.

Page 55 : "*Joys Seven.*"—There is an older carol of a similar sort, entitled, "Joyis Fyve."

Page 58 : "*The Moon shines bright.*"—Robert Bell, in his "Songs of the Peasantry " (1857), gives a May-day song (which used to be sung at Hitchin), containing some of the stanzas found in this carol.   Here is the song—

> " Remember us poor Mayers all !
>   And thus do we begin
> To lead our lives in righteous ways,
>   Or else we die in sin.
>
> We have been rambling all the night
>   And almost all the day ;
> And now returned back again,
>   We have brought you a branch of May.

A branch of May we have brought you,
And at your door it stands ;
   It is but a sprout,
   But it's well budded out
By the work of our Lord's hands.

The hedges and trees they are so green,
   As green as any leek ;
Our heavenly Father he watered them
   With his heavenly dew so sweet :

The heavenly gates are open wide,
   Our paths are beaten plain ;
And if a man be not too far gone,
   He may return again.

The life of man is but a span,
   It flourishes like a flower ;
We are here to-day and gone to-morrow,
   And we are dead in an hour.

The moon shines bright and the stars give a light,
   A little before it is day;
So God bless you all, both great and small,
   And send you a joyful May ! "

Page 68 : " *The contest of the Ivy and the Holly.*"—The two follownig pieces are from Wright's "Songs and Carols," published by the Percy Society :—

" *Hallelujah, hallelujah, hallelujah now sing we !*

   Here comes holly that is so gent,
   To please all men in his intent.
                 Hallelujah.

   But Lord and Lady of this hall,
   Whosoever against holly call,—
                 Hallelujah.

Whosoever against holly do cry,
In a lepe [1] shall he hang full high.
Hallelujah.

Whosoever against holly do sing,
He may weep and handès wring.
Hallelujah."

" Holly and ivy made a great party
Who should have the mastery
In lands where, they go.

Then spake Holly, I am free and jolly,
I will have the mastery,
In lands where they go.

Then spake Ivy, I am loud and proud,
And I will have the mastery
In lands where they go.

Then spake Holly and set him down on his knee,
I pray thee, gentle Ivy, say me no villany,
In lands where they go."

There is a modern carol of *The Holly and the Ivy*, frequently printed during the last hundred years. I give it from a broadside printed in the last century by T. Bloomer of Birmingham :—

" The holly and the ivy
Now are both well grown :
Of all the trees that are in the wood
The holly bears the crown.

Chorus.—The rising of the sun,
The running of the deer,
The playing of the merry organ,
Sweet singing in the choir.

---

[1] A large basket.

The holly bears a blossom
  As white as the lily flower ;
And Mary bore sweet Jesus Christ
  To be our sweet Saviour.

The holly bears a berry,
  As red as any blood ;
And Mary bore sweet Jesus Christ
  To do poor sinners good.

The holly bears a prickle,
  As sharp as any thorn ;
And Mary bore sweet Jesus Christ
  On Christmas-day in the morn.

The holly bears a bark,
  As bitter as any gall ;
And Mary bore sweet Jesus Christ
  For to redeem us all.

The holly and the ivy
  Now are both well grown :
Of all the trees that are in the wood
  The holly bears the crown."

Page 71 : "*Modryb Marya.*"—The figure of the noble-hearted vicar of Morwenstow stands out with striking picturesqueness. Had he been a border-minstrel in the old tumultuous days, he would surely have written many a ballad that the world would not willingly let die. His poems are few and unequal ; the best are singularly precious.

Page 75 : "*The shepherds went their hasty way.*"—Few great poets have written more execrably than Coleridge, when he is at his worst. His carol begins well ; but nothing more

R

inappropriate could be conceived than the reference to "The
maiden's love-confessing sigh," "War is a ruffian," &c. The
carol was written in 1799, two years after the peerless Kubla
Khan and the first part of Christabel.

Page 80 : "*Masters, in this hall.*"—In Sedding's "Antient
Christmas Carols" this carol is said to be translated from the
French.

Page 103 : "*Who can forget,*" &c.—These stanzas are taken
from the speech of Mercy towards the close of "Christ's
Victorie in Heaven," the first part of "Christ's Victorie and
Triumph in Heaven, and Earth, over, and after Death," first
published in 1610. The poem is full of striking and magnificent
imagery, expressed in richly-glowing jewelled stanzas. Milton
was a close student of Giles Fletcher.

Page 106 : "*The Shepherds.*"—Henry Vaughan, called "the
Silurist," from the fact that he was born among the Silures or
people of South Wales, is incomparably the greatest of English
devotional poets. The pieces that I have quoted, fine as they
are, do not give the reader a just idea of his greatness. Who-
ever will study Silex Scintillans as it deserves to be studied,
read it through and through again and again, cannot fail to be
deeply impressed by the magical beauty of the diction, the
perfect success with which the most difficult metrical effects
are lightly produced, the imaginative splendour and subtlety.
Vaughan was no less a born poet than Shelley or Keats or
Coleridge. He was born in 1621, and died in 1695. The
first part of Silex Scintillans was published in 1651 ; the
complete collection in two parts appeared in 1655. "Olor
Iscanus. A Collection of some select Poems and Translations.
Formerly written by Henry Vaughan, Silurist," was published
by the author's friends in 1651 ; it is far inferior to the volume

of sacred poems. Vaughan published nothing after 1655. Dr.
Grosart has edited a complete edition of Vaughan's writings.

Page 111 : "*New Prince, New Pomp.*"—A very quaint and
tender little poem. Another piece, entitled "New Heaven,
New War," is perhaps almost too quaint for modern readers ;
yet I venture to quote it in full :—

> " Come to your heaven, you heavenly quires !
> Earth hath the heaven of your desires ;
> Remove your dwelling to your God,
> A stall is now his best abode ;
> Sith men their homage do deny,
> Come, angels, all their fault supply.
>
> His chilling cold doth heat require,
> Come, seraphims, in lieu of fire ;
> This little ark no cover hath,
> Let cherubs' wings his body swathe ;
> Come, Raphael, this babe must eat,
> Provide our little Toby meat.
>
> Let Gabriel be now his groom,
> That first took up his earthly room ;
> Let Michael stand in his defence,
> Whom love hath linked to feeble sense ;
> Let Graces rock when he doth cry,
> And angels sing his lullaby.
>
> The same you saw in heavenly seat
> Is he that now sucks Mary's teat ;
> Agnize your King a mortal wight,
> His borrowed weed lets not your sight ;
> Come kiss the manger where he lies,
> That is your bliss above the skies.

This little Babe so few days old
Is come to rifle Satan's fold ;
All hell doth at his presence quake,
Though he himself for cold do shake ;
For in this weak unarmèd wise
The gates of hell he will surprise.

With tears he fights and wins the field,
His naked breast stands for a shield ;
His battering shots are babish cries ;
His arrows, looks of weeping eyes ;
His martial ensigns, cold and need ;
And feeble flesh his warrior's steed.

His camp is pitchèd in a stall,
His bulwark but a broken wall ;
The crib his trench, hay-stalks his stakes ;
Of shepherds he his muster makes ;
And thus, as sure his foe to wound,
The angels' trumps alarum sound.

My soul, with Christ join thou in fight ;
Stick to the tents that he hath pight ;
Within his crib is surest ward,
This little Babe will be thy guard ;
If thou wilt foil thy foes with joy,
Then flit not from this Heavenly Boy."

I must also find room for the poem, entitled "The Burning Babe" :—

"As I in hoary winter's night stood shivering in the snow,
Surprised I was with sudden heat which made my heart to glow ;
And lifting up a fearful eye to view what fire was near,
A pretty babe all burning bright did in the air appear,

Who scorchèd with excessive heat such floods of tears did shed,
As though his floods should quench his flames which with his
    tears were fed.
Alas ! quoth he, but newly born in fiery heats I fry,
Yet none approach to warm their hearts or feel my fire but I !
My faultless breast the furnace is, the fuel wounding thorns ;
Love is the fire and sighs the smoke, the ashes shame and scorns ;
The fuel Justice layeth on, and Mercy blows the coals ;
The metal in this furnace wrought are men's defilèd souls ;
For which, as now on fire I am, to work them to their good,
So will I melt into a bath to wash them in my blood.
With that he vanish'd out of sight and swiftly shrunk away,
And straight I callèd unto mind that it was Christmas Day."

Ben Jonson told Drummond of Hawthornden that he would
have been content to destroy many of his own writings if he
had written " The Burning Babe."

Southwell's longest poem, "St. Peter's Complaint," is
smoothly written, but tedious. After three years' close impri-
sonment in the Tower, Southwell was executed at Tyburn, on
February 22, 1594-5, at the age of thirty-four or thirty-five.
Though he was found guilty of treasonable practices, his sole
offence was that he had been a zealous priest of the Church of
Rome. He appears to have been a man of noble character,
humble and gentle and intrepid. [In the last line of the penultimate stanza of " New Prince, New Pomp," the word *praisèd*
should be *prizèd*. I quoted from an inaccurate reprint.]

Page 113 : *"All after pleasures as I rid one day."*—These
lines are very characteristic of the polished high-born scholar,
who, after strenuous attempts to gain preferment at court,
abandoned at length the fruitless quest and found content in the
retirement of a country vicarage. Herbert is a soothing writer ;
his Muse took an equable steady flight, never soaring into the

"highest heaven of invention," but yet keeping at a respectable distance from the ground. He numbers at least ten readers for Vaughan's one,—a fact which is not at all surprising.

Page 115: "*Immortal Babe,*" &c.—From "The Shaking of the Olive Tree," 1660. Joseph Hall, Bishop of Exeter, was born in 1574, and died on 8th September 1656. He was an eloquent, liberal-minded, witty, and bold divine. He was also one of our earliest English satirists.

Page 116: "*The Shepherd's Song.*"—This piece is subscribed "E. B." in the original editions (1600 and 1614) of "England's Helicon." Other pieces in that delightful collection bear the name "Edmund Bolton" in full; so doubtless we are right in giving the present poem to Bolton. In the early editions the two last lines are printed thus:—

> "In *Dauid's* Cittie dooth this Sunne appeare :
> Clouded in flesh, yet Sheepheards sit we heere."

My punctuation seems preferable. Bolton is known as a poet only from his contributions to "England's Helicon."

Page 120: "*A Hymn of the Nativity.*"—This poem strikingly exhibits Crashaw's power and weakness. Thrice-refined golden speech, a subtle sense of melody, fervid richness of imagination, —these great gifts were marred by a constant indulgence in violent conceits, by diffuseness, and occasionally by studied harshness of phrase and rhythm. The second piece, "Hymn for the Epiphany," offends so outrageously by ill-timed conceits, that I have only printed the first part of it, although there are many fine lines in the latter part. Crashaw was driven from Cambridge at the time of the Civil Wars; escaped to France, embraced the Catholic faith, and afterwards became secretary to Cardinal Palotta at Rome. He died at Loretto in 1650 (at the age of thirty-seven) ; and it has been supposed that he was poisoned. His poems were published in 1646 under the title of " Steps to the Temple," and "The Delights of the Muses."

Page 128: "*Run, shepherds, run,*" &c.—Too often in read- ing Drummond of Hawthornden we feel that the poet is giving us "words, words, words." His work is always polished and refined, but seldom throbs with life. The two sonnets I have quoted are graceful but (it must be confessed) commonplace. There is an elaborate life of Drummond (who died in 1649) by Professor Masson.

Page 130 : " *Of the Epiphany.*"—Sir John Beaumont was an elder brother of Francis Beaumont the dramatist. Drayton, in his Epistle to Henry Reynolds, couples the brothers together in terms of genial praise :—

"Then the two Beaumonts and my Browne arose,
My dear companions whom I freely chose
My bosom friends ; and in their several ways
Rightly born poets, and in these last days
Men of much note and no less nobler parts,
Such as have freely told to me their hearts,
As I have mine to them."

John Beaumont was created a baronet in 1626 and died in 1628, ætat. 44. He is the author of " Bosworth Field and other Poems " (posthumously printed in 1629), which have been praised by Wordsworth for their "spirit, elegance, and har- mony."

Page 132: " *Where is this blessed Babe ?* "—Jeremy Taylor, whose prose is one of the glories of English literature, handles his lyre awkwardly. At starting we are confronted with a false rhyme ; and as we proceed we feel that the versification is wanting in ease and fluency. What a change when we turn to the perfect prose-periods of the funeral sermon on the Countess of Carbery !

Page 136 : "*And they laid him in a manger.*"—Sir Edward Sherburne came of an ancient Lancashire family ; he was born in 1616, and is supposed to have died in 1702. He made a translation of Manilius and of some plays of Seneca. When the Civil Wars broke out he sided with the King's party and lost his fortune. He was knighted by Charles the Second.

Page 140 : "*Rejoice, rejoice, with heart and voice.*"—The author, Francis Kinwelmersh, was a member of Gray's Inn. He had a brother Antony, who also wrote verse.

Page 143 : "*Sleep, baby, sleep.*"—This *Christmas Lullaby* has not been printed before.

Page 145 : "*A Rocking Hymn.*"—Wither's besetting fault is his prolixity ; he seldom knew when to stop. It is tedious to read through the voluminous list of his forgotten writings, but to read the works themselves is a Herculean task. Yet every student of English poetry knows that some of Wither's songs are miracles of sweetness, and that even in his most arid wastes of prose and verse there are green oases. It is much to be wished that some capable scholar would make an anthology from Wither. From the cradle hymn I ventured to omit the second stanza, which ran thus :—

"Though thy conception was in sin,
A sacred bathing thou hast had ;
And though thy birth unclean hath bin,
A blameless babe thou now art made :
Sweet baby, then, forbear to weep ;
Be still, my dear ; sweet baby, sleep."

The piece would be improved by making a few more omissions.
Not so with the carol which follows, written in Wither's blithest
strain, perfect from first to last.

Page 151 : " *Now poor men to the justices.*"—The old poet
Gascoigne tells us that tenants used to take their landlords
presents on Quarter-Day :

" And when the tenants come to pay their quarter's rent,
   They bring some fowl at Midsummer, a dish of fish in Lent ;
   At Christmas a capon, at Michaelmas a goose ;
   And somewhat else at New-Year's tide, *for fear their lease flie
   loose.*"

Page 152 : " *The wild mare in is bringing.*"—The game of
"shoeing the wild mare." A youth was chosen to be the wild
mare : he was allowed a start, and the other players then pursued
him with the object of shoeing him. From Strutt's meagre description it appears to have been a poor sport. I suppose that
in the attempt to escape from the pursuers the wild mare kicked
out lustily, upsetting chairs and tables. I don't know what
game is meant in the previous line, " The boys are come to
catch the owls." In the next stanza "noddy" is an old game
of cards resembling cribbage. Of the game of "Rowland-ho"
I can find no particulars.

Page 154 : " *With the last year's brand,*" &c.—When a piece
of last year's Christmas log was preserved, the household
reckoned itself secure from the assaults of hobgoblins, as Herrick elsewhere relates :—

      " Kindle the Christmas brand, and then
            Till sunset let it burn ;
         Which quenched, then lay it up again
            Till Christmas next return.

> Part must be kept wherewith to teend
>   The Christmas log next year;
> And where 'tis safely kept, the fiend
>   Can do no mischief there."

Page 156 : " *Wassail the trees.*"—This custom was kept up till the end of the last century.   Brand relates that in 1790 a Cornish man informed him it was the custom for the Devonshire people on the eve of Twelfth Day to go after supper into the orchard with a large milk-pan full of cyder with roasted apples in it.   Each person took what was called a clayen cup, *i.e.* an earthenware cup full of cyder, and standing under each of the more fruitful trees, sung—

> " Health to thee, good apple-tree,
>   Well to bear, pocket-fulls, hat-fulls,
>   Peck-fulls, bushel-bag-fulls."

After drinking part of the contents of the cup, he threw the rest, with the fragments of the roasted apples, at the trees, amid the shouting of the company.   Another song sung on such occasions was :—

> " Here's to thee, old apple-tree,
> Whence thou may'st bud, and whence thou may'st blow,
> And whence thou may'st bear apples enow !
>   Hats full ! caps full !
>   Bushel-bushel-sacks full,
>   And my pockets full, too, huzza ! "

It is supposed that the custom was a relic of the sacrifice to Pomona.

Page 163 : " *March beer.*"—Harrison, in his " Description of England," ii. 6, says :—" The beer that is used at noblemen's tables in their fixed and standing houses is commonly of a year old, or peradventure of two years' tunning or more, but this is not general. *It is also brewed in March, and therefore called March beer;* but for the household it is usually not under a month's age, each one coveting to have the same stale as he may, so that it be not sour, and his bread as new as possible, so that it be not hot."

Page 168 : " *O you merry, merry souls.*"—These lively verses, with some additions and alterations, are also found in an undated collection of songs entitled "The Hop Garland."—Last year the enterprising publishers, Messrs. Field & Tuer, issued a reprint of " Round about the Coal Fire."

Page 170: " *Caput apri defero.*"—There is still another Boar's-head Carol, in addition to those in pp. 170–2. Ritson first printed it (from Add. MS. 5665, the valuable folio which he presented to the British Museum) :—

" Nowell, nowell, nowell, nowell,
    Tidings good I think to tell.
The boar's head that we bring here
Betokeneth a prince without peer,
Is born this day to buy us dear,
              Nowell.

A boar is a sovran beast,
And acceptable in every feast,
So mote this lord be to most and least,
              Nowell.

This boar's head we bring with song,
In worship of him that thus sprung
Of a virgin to redress all wrong,
              Nowell."

Page 173 : " *May both with manchet stand replete.*"—*Manchet* was fine wheaten bread.

Page 176: "*A jolly wassail bowl.*"—The undated black-letter "New Christmas Carols," from which this piece is taken, is bound up with three other collections of Christmas verses. The volume, which is in the Bodleian Library, formerly belonged to Antony-à-Wood. Each tract numbers only a few 12mo pages. In the same little volume is a curious prose-tract on the Arraignment of Christmas.

Page 183: "*Here we come a whistling.*"—Another correspondent of *Notes and Queries* mentions that at Harrington in Worcestershire it was customary for children on St. Thomas's Day (December 21) to go round the village begging for apples, and singing—

> " Wassail, wassail through the town,
>   If you've got any apples throw them down ;
>   Up with the stocking and down with the shoe,
>   If you've got no apples money will do ;
>   The jug is white and the ale is brown,
>   This is the best house in the town."

An Oxfordshire lady tells me that at her house near Witney the village children sing on Christmas-eve—

> " Holly and ivy, tickle my toe,
>   Give me a red apple and let me go ;
>   Give me another for my little brother,
>   And I'll go home to my father and my mother."

A writer in *Current Notes* for January 1856 gives the following verses :—

> " I wish you a merry Christmas
>   And a happy New Year,
>   A pocket full of money,
>   And a cellar full of beer,[a]
>   And a good fat pig to serve you all the year.

Ladies and gentlemen, sat by the fire,
Pity we poor boys out in the mire."

In Oxfordshire the children sing the first four lines of this
piece, and then proceed :—

"All the roads are very dirty,
My boots are very thin;
I've got a little pocket,
Will you put a penny in ? "

Page 190: "*At hot cockles beside.*"—In the game of *hot cockles*
one of the players, after being blindfolded, laid his head in
another's lap. The rest proceeded in turn to strike the blindfolded victim, until he was released from his position by
guessing the name of the person who struck him. In Strutt's
"Sports and Pastimes" (ed. 1801, p. 293) there is an illustration
of this ancient sport from a fifteenth-century illuminated MS.

Page 214 : "*Provide for Christmas.*"—*Poor Robin's Almanac,*
from which this and other pieces are taken, began in 1663 and
ended in 1776. No public or private library, so far as I know,
possesses a complete set of these very interesting almanacs.
It has been stated that Robert Herrick was the original pro-
jector of the series, but I believe there is no authority for the
statement. "Poor Robin" was the *nom de plume* of Robert
Winstanley of Saffron Walden, a list of whose publications is
given by Mr. H. Eckroyd Smith in *Notes and Queries,* ser. vi.
vol. 7, pp. 321-3. More information about Poor Robin is very
much needed. .

Page 225 : "*Right wantonly a mumming.*"—Christmas mumming still continues in many parts of the country, but it is only
the shadow of its former self. A few years ago it was kept up
at Chiswick. Robert Bell (in "Songs of the Peasantry") gives an

amusing Mummer's Song that used to be sung in the neighbourhood of Richmond, Yorkshire, by a rustic actor dressed as an
old horse.   One verse in a Somersetshire Mummer's song is
very droll :—

> "Here comes I, liddle man Jan,
>   With my zword in my hand !
>   If you don't all do
>   As you be told by I,
>   I'll zend you all to York
>   For to make apple-pie."

My fair Oxfordshire correspondent writes:—" The mummers
still go round to the farm-houses at home, but their glory has
departed.   I can remember being immensely pleased with their
acting, and remember one little bit they said which always
took my fancy.   One fellow would shout out, ' Come in, Jack
Spinner !'   Then in came Jack Spinner, saying :—

> ' Yer comes I as an't bin it,
>   We my gret yead and little wit.'
>
> (*i.e.* Here come I that haven't been yet
>   With my great head and little wit.) "

In "Round about our Coal Fire" we read :—" Then comes
Mumming or Masquerading, when the squire's wardrobe is
ransacked for dresses of all kinds, and the coal-hole searched
around, or corks burnt to black the faces of the fair or make
deputy-moustaches; and every one in the family except the
squire himself must be transformed from what they were."

Page 227 : *Of ash-heaps, in the which ye use,*" &c.—William
Browne (in one of his sonnets to Celia) alludes to this curious
mode of divination :—

" If, forced by our sighs, the flame shall fly
Of our kind love and get within thy rind,
Be wary, gentle Bay, and shriek not high
When thou dost such unusual fervour find :
Suppress the fire, for, should it take thy leaves,
Their crackling would betray us and thy glory."

Works, ed. Hazlitt, ii. 288.

[In line 13, for " Quite *though* " read " Quite *through*."]

Page 229 : " *Where bean's the king of the sport here.*"—A bean
and pea were enclosed in the Twelfth-cake. When the cake
was divided, he who got the slice containing the bean was king
of the feast, and the girl to whose lot the pea fell was queen.
This Twelfth-tide custom existed in France as early as the
thirteenth century. See some interesting remarks in the preface
to Sandys' Christmas Carols (pp. lxxvi.–ix.)

Page 230 : "*With gentle lambs-wool.*"—*Lambs-wool* consisted
of strong nappy ale, in which roasted crab-apples were pressed.
Nares conjectures that the name was derived from the liquor's
"smoothness and softness, resembling the wool of lambs."

Page 231 : " *Christmas in the Olden Time.*"—It may not be
amiss here to quote a lengthy passage, relating to Christmas
observances, from the fourth book of Barnabe Googe's " Popish
Kingdom," (1570), a translation of Thomas Kirchmaier's [Nao-
georgus'] " Regnum Papisticum " (1553). The writer is describ-
ing the customs observed in Germany ;.but in many respects the
description would be equally applicable to English society in the
middle of the sixteenth century :—

" Three weeks before the day whereon was born the Lord of
grace,
And on the Thursday boys and girls do run in every place,
And bounce and beat at every door, with blows and lusty snaps
And cry, the advent of the Lord, not born as yet perhaps :

And wishing to the neighbours all, that in the houses dwell,
A happy year, and everything to spring and prosper well :
Here have they pears and plums, and pence, each man gives
　　willingly,
For these three nights are always thought unfortunate to be :
Wherein they are afraid of sprites and cankered witches' spite,
And dreadful devils black and grim, that then have chiefest
　　might.
In these same days young wanton girls that meet for marriage be,
Do search to know the names of them that shall their husbands
　　be.
Four onions, five, or eight, they take, and make in every one
Such names as they do fancy most and best do think upon.
Thus near the chimney then they set, and that same onion than
The first doth sprout doth surely bear the name of their good
　　man.
Their husband's nature eke they seek to know and all his
　　guise ;
When as the sun hath hid himself, and left the starry skies,
Unto some woodstack do they go, and while they there do
　　stand,
Each one draws out a faggot stick, the next that comes to hand,
Which if it straight and even be, and have no knots at all,
A gentle husband then they think shall surely to them fall.
But if it foul and crooked be, and knotty here and there,
A crabbed churlish husband then they earnestly do fear.
These things the wicked Papists bear, and suffer willingly,
Because they neither do the end, nor fruits of faith espie :
And rather had the people should obey their foolish lust,
Than truly God to know, and in him here alone to trust.
　　Then comes the day wherein the Lord did bring his birth to
　　　pass,
Whereas at midnight up they rise, and every man to Mass.

This time so holy counted is, that divers earnestly
Do think the waters all to wine are changed suddenly :
In that same hour that Christ himself was born, and came to
    light,
And unto water straight again transformed and altered quite.
There are beside that mindfully the money still do watch,
That first to altar comes, which then they privily do snatch.
The priests lest other should it have takes oft the same away,
Whereby they think throughout the year to have good luck in
    play,
And not to lose : then straight at game till daylight do they
    strive,
To make some present proof how well their hallowed pence will
    thrive.
Three masses every priest doth sing upon that solemn day,
With offerings unto every one, that so the more may play.
This done, a wooden child in clouts is on the altar set,
About the which both boys and girls do dance and trimly jet,
And carols sing in praise of Christ, and for to help them here,
The organs answer every verse, with sweet and solemn cheer.
The priests do roar aloud, and round about the parents stand,
To see the sport, and with their voice do help them and their
    hand.
Thus wont the Coribants perhaps upon the mountain Ide,
The crying noise of Jupiter new born with song to hide,
To dance about him round, and on their brazen pans to beat,
Lest that his father finding him, should him destroy and eat.
   Then followeth Saint Stephen's Day, whereon doth every
    man
His horses jaunt and course abroad, as swiftly as he can.
Until they do extremely sweat, and then they let them blood,
For this being done upon this day, they say doth do them
    good,

S

And keeps them from all maladies and sickness through the
　　year,
As if that Stephen any time took charge of horses here.
　　Next John the son of Zebedee hath his appointed day,
Who once by cruel tyrant's will constrained was, they say,
Strong poison up to drink, therefore the Papists do believe,
That whoso puts their trust in him, no poison them can grieve.
The wine beside that hallowed is, in worship of his name,
The priests do give the people that bring money for the same.
And after with the selfsame wine are little manchets made,
Against the boisterous winter storms, and sundry such like
　　trade;
The men upon this solemn day do take this holy wine,
To make them strong, so do the maids to make them fair and
　　fine.
　　Then comes the day that calls to mind the cruel Herod's
　　strife,
Who seeking Christ to kill, the King of everlasting life,
Destroyed the infants young, a beast unmerciless,
And put to death all such as were of two years age or less.
To them the sinful wretches cry, and earnestly do pray
To get them pardon for their faults, and wipe their sins away.
The parents when this day appears, do beat their children all
(Though nothing they deserve), and servants all to beating fall.
And monks do whip each other well, or else their Prior great,
Or Abbot mad, doth take in hand their breeches all to beat
In worship of these Innocents, or rather as we see,
In honour of the cursed king that did this cruelty.
　　The next to this is New Year's Day, whereon to every friend
They costly presents in do bring and New Year's gifts do
　　send.
These gifts the husband gives his wife and father eke the child,
And master on his men bestows the like, with favour mild,

And good beginning of the year they wish and wish again,
According to the ancient guise of heathen people vain.
These eight days no man doth require his debts of any man,
Their tables do they furnish out with all the meat they can :
With marchpanes, tarts, and custards great they drink with
    staring eyes,
They rout and revel, feed and feast as merry all as pies,
As if they should at the entrance of this New Year have to die,
Yet would they have their bellies full and ancient friends ally.

   The wise men's day here followeth, who out from Persia far,
Brought gifts and presents unto Christ, conducted by a star.
The Papists do believe that these were kings, and so them call,
And do affirm that of the same there were but three in all.
Here sundry friends together come, and meet in company,
And make a king amongst themselves by voice or destiny ;
Who after princely guise appoints his officers alway,
Then unto feasting do they go, and long time after play :
Upon their boards in order thick the dainty dishes stand,
Till that their purses empty be and creditors at hand.
Their children herein follow them, and choosing princes here,
With pomp and great solemnity, they meet and make good
    cheer
With money either got by stealth, or of their parents eft,
That so they may be trained to know both riot here and theft.
Then also every householder to his ability,
Doth make a mighty cake, that may suffice his company :
Herein a penny doth he put, before it come to fire,
This he divides according as his household doth require ;
And every piece distributeth, as round about they stand,
Which in their names unto the poor is given out of hand ;
But whoso chanceth on the piece wherein the money lies
Is counted king amongst them all, and is with shouts and
    cries

Exalted to the heavens up, who taking chalk in hand,
Doth make a cross on every beam and rafters as they stand :
Great force and power have these against all injuries and
    harms
Of cursed devils, sprites and bugs, of conjurings and charms.
So much this king can do, so much the crosses bring to pass,
Made by some servant, maid or child, or by some foolish ass.
Twice six nights then from Christmas they do count with dili-
    gence,
Wherein each master in his house doth burn up frankincense :
And on the table sets a loaf, when night approacheth near,
Before the coals, and frankincense to be perfumed there :
First bowing down his head he stands, and nose and ears and
    eyes,
He smokes and with his mouth receive[s] the fume that doth
    arise :
Whom followeth straight his wife, and doth the same full solemnly,
And of their children every one, and all their family :
Which doth preserve they say their teeth, and nose, and eyes,
    and ear,
From every kind of malady, and sickness all the year.
When every one received hath this odour great and small,
Then one takes up the pan with coals, and frankincense and
    all.
Another takes the loaf, whom all the rest do follow here,
And round about the house they go, with torch or taper clear,
That neither bread nor meat do want, nor witch with dreadful
    charm
Have power to hurt their children, or to do their cattle harm.
.There are that three nights only do perform this foolish gear,
To this intent, and think themselves in safety all the year.
To Christ dare none commit himself.   And in these days beside
They judge what weather all the year shall happen and betide :

Ascribing to each day a month, and at this present time
The youth in every place do flock, and, all appareled fine,
With pipers through the streets they run, and sing at every door
In commendation of the man rewarded well therefore,
Which on themselves they do bestow, or on the church, as tho'
The people were not plagued with rogues and begging friars
    enow.
There cities are where boys and girls together still do run,
About the street with like, as soon as night begins to come,
And bring abroad their wassail bowls, who well rewarded be
With cakes and cheese and great good cheer and money plen-
    teously.

   Page 239 : *"Mark well my heavy doleful tale."*—Christmas
festivities were not wholly ended on Twelfth day. The 7th of
January, Distaff day (otherwise called Rock day), was given
up partly to business and partly to play, as Herrick tells us in
the following dainty poem (two lines of which I am forced to
omit) :—

> "Partly work and partly play
> Ye must on Saint Distaff's day,
> From the plough soon free your team,
> Then come home and fodder them.
> If the maids a-spinning go,
> Burn the flax and fire the tow.
>
> .   .   .   .   .
> .   .   .   .   .
>
> Bring in pails of water then,
> Let the maids bewash the men.
> Give Saint Distaff all the right,
> Then bid Christmas sport good night ;
> And next morrow, every one
> To his own vocation."

On Candlemas day, the 2nd of February, the holly and ivy were taken down, and all traces of Christmas disappeared, as Herrick tells us in his Ceremonies for Candlemas Eve. *Lector benevole, vale.*

> Yule's come and Yule's gane,
>   And we have feasted weel;
> Sae Jock maun to his flail again,
>   And Jenny to her wheel.

FINIS.